The Willow Tree

The Willow Tree

By

Helen Nardecchia

Katy Crossing Press

The Willow Tree
By Helen Nardecchia
Georgetown, TX
http://www.helennardecchia.com/

Published by Katy Crossing Press
Georgetown, Texas
http://www.katycrossingpress.com

Copyright © 2011 Helen Nardecchia
ISBN-13: 978-0-9849684-0-4
ISBN-10: 0984968407

Watercolor cover by Addie Busfield

Dedication:
To my grandchildren - -
"Listen to the words in your heart
and write a story"

A special thank you to my husband, Bud, and daughter, Karen Barry, who took the time to read every sentence and page before publishing, and especially Ann Bell, my editor, who made all of this possible."

Other books by Helen Nardecchia

Sophie and Ben: A Family Love Story

Remembering the Early Years

One

Up earlier than usual this morning, Mary Bryant Clark pulled her white vintage Mustang into her reserved parking space at the newspaper. A smile crossed her face as she thought about Reed Lowell. She met him only once when he toured the newspaper to introduce himself to all its employees. With only a quick glance, she guessed he might be around thirty-four, but his tall, lean appearance and crop of brown hair made him look younger. His brilliant smile as he shook hands with employees flashed in her mind.

As she climbed the brick stairs of the large, gray building, The Lowell Report, in big gold letters, sparkled in the morning sunshine. It had not lost its brilliance since installed. She hurried along, anxious to be in place at the conference table before Reed appeared. As she passed her office before heading to the conference room, she peeked in and saw Patty typing at her desk.

"Morning, Patty. Any new developments before I head for the conference room?"

Turning quickly, Patty smiled, "Good

morning, Mary. You may want to see the memo on your desk before going. There are other messages, but they can wait until after the meeting."

A memo, signed by Reed, sat on Mary's desk. A personnel change was mentioned, and she found herself speaking louder than intended, "Personnel change? Well, this should certainly peak everyone's interest" She hoped Patty didn't hear her.

When Mary entered the conference room, she could see that all departments were well represented. Even Tony Weiss, who managed the press room showed up. Boy, that's a first, thought Mary. He usually sends someone else. The only one not there, so far, was Reed Lowell. As Mary pulled out a chair to sit down, she leaned over and quietly said to Dave Becker, head of Editorials, "Where's the boss?"

Busily jotting down notes on a tablet, Dave looked up and said, "His secretary said he is running late and we should start without him. She is getting ready to read the minutes from the last meeting."

Susie Parker, Reed's secretary, called the meeting to order. Shortly after she read the Minutes, Reed arrived. He greeted everyone and took his seat at the head of the conference table. On Reed's right sat Phoebe Lowell, Reed's mother, with gray hair piled high and pulled back into a bun.

She was seventy-seven years old and never missed a monthly meeting. Mary saw the strong resemblance between the two. She remembered the day Susie gave her the tour of the building when she was hired as a reporter in the journalist pool.

"That's Phoebe Lowell, Reed's mother and that's his father, Stephen Lowell," Susie said, as she pointed to each portrait hanging in the foyer of the company. "Reed became Executive Director after his father passed away five years ago. Stephen Lowell had a wonderful reputation. He was loved by all and Reed seems to be following in his father's footsteps."

After the tour, Mary wondered what part Phoebe Lowell played in the success of the newspaper. She wondered until one of the employees in the Data and Statistics Department related at lunch how Phoebe encouraged Reed at the time to take the company over. "She told him she'd help him in every way she could. And she did. I've been here a long time and," said the employee, "after two years, Phoebe delights in the fact that the newspaper is sailing smoothly on calm waters. Most of the staff feels their jobs and the company are secure with Reed and his mother at the helm."

A good feeling surged through Mary after her conversation with Susie. She felt confident she had made a wise choice applying for a job at The Lowell Report. If Phoebe and the people of Rockford, Illinois have that much confidence in her son and his ingenuity, then I will also. I'll bet Phoebe has had complete confidence in him from his little boy days and on.

Mary's mind returned to the conference when she heard Reed say, "Before we get into each department's progress report, I want to read part of an article I found very interesting. It's from a Dallas newspaper I picked up at the airport this morning.

"Journalism is different today. The lines have blurred between reporter and talk-show host, between respectable newspaper and scandal sheet, between politician and commentator, between information and entertainment. In the fevered competition among multiple channels, every minute is a deadline and every rumor is a story.

Is what we once called journalism to be replaced by storytelling for fun and profit?"

Reed stopped reading and let the words sink in. The silence was deafening. No one even shuffled papers. Finally, after a few minutes, he said, "I took the liberty of copying the article for each of you to read and re-read often as a reminder that we have a duty to our country and the American people to be honest and straightforward; to do our best to write and print events that actually happened and avoid putting our own interpretations and opinions before the public. Every story has characters, action, sometimes violence, sometimes happiness and it is our job to only listen attentively, and present the facts in written form for others to supply their own interpretations and opinions. Please frame it and hang it somewhere in your office. When you think you have gone beyond the line of duty, read it again!"

As Susie passed out the copies, Reed said, "Now, let's start with you Dave. Give us your progress report."

The meeting was coming to a close when Reed finally said, "There will be a couple of changes in personnel. Phoebe Lowell is going to be in charge of the Data and Statistics Department effective immediately. When the newspaper began in 1940, Phoebe and my father worked diligently to present the highest standards in local and government news. He placed her in charge of researching incoming statistical information and I think we will do that again. No data or statistics are to be written into articles or printed until approval by her. We have had to place correction boxes in The Lowell Report a few too many times because of statistics quoted incorrectly."

Mary scanned the room and spotted a frown on Murray Adams's face. Looking down at her notes, she smiled knowing

Murray, Superintendent of Data and Statistics, would not be happy having to answer to Phoebe. It's well known Murray doesn't like to answer to anyone.

"Also," continued Reed, "Liz Turner has given notice this morning that she's leaving in two weeks. Her husband has been transferred to Los Angeles and we wish them both the best of luck. Liz has certainly been an asset to our newspaper. She has done a splendid job on the Life & Arts section. We will need a replacement and ask those interested to see Susie after the meeting. Each will be interviewed and then a decision made."

Fifteen minutes were allowed for suggestions and updates. Dave Becker, Sports Coordinator, spoke first. "This year's Golf Tournament will be held Saturday, June 5th at Aldeen Golf Course, and all proceeds will go to United Way. Attendance last year was overwhelming with three hundred people teeing off. Since everyone had such a good time, we ask that you consider it again this year."

"What's on the menu this year, Dave?" someone shouted from the back of the room.

"What'd you think of the menu last year?" Dave asked.

Eyes glistened, eyebrows raised and some rubbed tummies making it an all-round approval rating so Dave said, "Well, you'll probably get the same thing again."

Laughter filled the room.

Murray Adams stood up next and gave his report on Rockford's labor force.

"As of August, 1970, employment was at 190,519. Number unemployed 7,122, with 3.1% unemployed. This is the lowest percentage in ten years, and the economy is good."

Murray continued with a listing of non-agricultural wage and salary workers statistics, beginning with construction and mining and ending with government.

After all had given their reports, the meeting was adjourned. Reed gathered up his papers, shoved them in his briefcase and stood to leave. Dave Becker walked over and detained him a few minutes. Mary found herself watching Reed as he smiled and conversed with Dave. She liked what she saw and learned through the office grapevine that Reed wasn't married. She could not imagine why. She found him very attractive.

But he was not the reason she decided to apply for Liz Turner's position. She gathered up her papers spread out on the conference table and walked over to Susie.

Mary had no objection to the journalist pool. Five other journalists shared the second floor with her. Each had their own office with polished paneling and tapestry drapes. She couldn't ask for a better secretary. Patty's efficiency amazed her at times. Lead stories were passed out in the morning and the pool people decided who would do what story. Some stories were juicy, some were dull. They could run anywhere from a break-in and robbery to a cat stuck in an exposed pipeline. It's just time to move up, thought Mary.

Susie was reading over the minutes of the morning when Mary approached her. Looking up, she said, "Hi, Mary, haven't seen you in a little while. How are you?"

"I'm fine, Susie, and you?"

"Very busy."

Mary hesitated a minute and then got right to the point. "Susie, I would like to apply for Liz's Life and Arts position."

"Okay, I've got some forms here in my briefcase. Just a minute, I'll get one out for you." Susie fumbled through her briefcase and finally brought out several forms she had printed early that morning. "The form is self-explanatory. Just fill it out and give it back to me. I'll see that Reed gets it."

Mary took the form and sat down at the conference table to fill it out. It was simple; name, address, telephone number, present department, salary and the question, "What qualification would you bring to the Life & Arts department?"

She filled out the form easily until she got

to the question. *I've got to make this good if I want this position*, she thought. And so she wrote. "In this year of 1970, I feel a strong desire and determination to bring the best photography, illustrations, information and interviews I know to the people of Rockford, Illinois. Life is a gift and the Arts are a bonus." Mary handed the form back to Susie.

Susie smiled and said, "Good luck. Depending upon how many others apply, we should be able to let you know within a couple of weeks."

Mary thanked her and left the conference room. When she returned to her office, there was a file on her desk. She opened it, realizing it was her next assignment. Cheryl Cunningham was getting married and she was to cover the entire affair. Photos were needed and a complete story from the time Cheryl opened her eyes in the morning until the last dance of the evening. The Cunningham's owned the Bank of Rockford which stood in the middle of the downtown area. They were the 'crème de la crème' of the local social world. A full page story was recommended in the file.

Mary pulled up the telephone book from the bottom shelf of her desk to locate the number. Running her finger down the last names under "C", she found it under Michael Cunningham, III, 6254 Charles

Street, 275-2000. She leaned over the telephone book and dialed the numbers.

A stiff voice said, "Mr. Cunningham's residence."

"This is Mary Bryant Clark from The Lowell Report and I wonder if I could speak with Cheryl Cunningham, please."

"Miss Cunningham is not available at the moment. May I take a message?"

"Yes," said Mary, "Would you have her call me at 555-3000?"

There was a moment of silence and then, "Who did you say was calling again?"

"Mary Bryant Clark from The Lowell Report newspaper."

"I will see that she gets your message, Madam."

Twenty minutes later the phone rang in Mary's office and the voice on the other end said, "This is Cheryl Cunningham. I have a message that Mary Bryant Clark called me. Is she there?"

"Yes, speaking. Miss Cunningham, I understand you are planning a wedding and The Lowell Report would like to do a full page story on the event, with your permission, of course."

Cheryl was dazzled. "Oh, Miss Clark, that would be lovely."

"Can we set up an appointment now for next week to go over all the particulars?"

"What day did you have in mind?"

"Well, let's see. My calendar tells me I have Wednesday of next week open. Would that work for you?"

Cheryl Cunningham was silent for a moment and then said, "I think that will be fine."

"Good, let's make it Wednesday at ten o'clock."

"Absolutely," answered Cheryl.

Mary thought this is too easy. Can't believe it. "Yes," said Mary "that will be perfect."

As Cheryl Cunningham began to sign off, Mary said, "Oh, by the way, Miss Cunningham, could I have the groom's name?"

"Why, of course, it's Reed Lowell."

Two

*C*heryl Cunningham's voice rang in Mary's ears. "Why, of course, it's Reed Lowell." Completely stunned, she had a hard time getting over Cheryl's casual remark. There went her plans for zeroing in on him.

Wednesday's meeting with Cheryl Cunningham was cancelled. Victor opened the front door with a message that an emergency came up and Cheryl would have to set up another date. "She intends to call you, Miss Bryant."

Mary accepted the message with annoyance. *She had my phone number. Why didn't she call?* As she drove to the office, she decided not to make an issue of it, but just call her and set up another date.

Her stomach growled. Checking her watch, she realized it was too early to have lunch. A small coffee shop on a nearby corner caught her eye, and she pulled into a parking place. A bell tinkled as she opened the door. After ordering and paying for a cup of black coffee and a chocolate donut, she selected a small corner booth in the back of the shop.

Mary stared out the window on the side of the booth. Seeing an older couple walking arm in arm, she thought of her mother, Grace, and her dad, Jed. More than once, comments were made on how much she resembled her mother. Both had the lovely auburn hair inherited from her maternal grandmother, Margaret Walker, and Mary hoped she'd age as gracefully as her mother did. Even with several streaks of gray through her mother's hair now, her deep blue eyes kept her young and vibrant looking.

"We share a common bond," Mary often told friends. "We love music." Sitting there, she almost laughed out loud when she thought about the huge Baldwin piano placed boldly and proudly in the center of the living room. It reminded her of Grandma Bryant, playing endlessly throughout an entire evening, performing all the songs she had ever learned as a child. At the end, she'd close the cover over the keys and not return again for several months or even a year.

Through Grace's insistence, Mary took lessons as a youngster for three or four years, only to please her mother who just didn't want to see the old piano collect dust. She blushed when she thought how her mind went blank at a recital one year. She simply stood up and walked away from the piano, and at Christmas time, it takes quite a bit of coaxing and a couple of glasses of wine for her to return to the piano bench.

She left the booth after the short snack with a smile on her face, and drove back to the office. She spent the rest of the day catching up on messages and phone calls.

* * *

When Mary's day ended at the office, she slipped into the driver's seat of her car and thought about the long ride home. The hour ride to Poplar Grove located in Boone County gave her time to think. The land where she lived was purchased by her paternal grandparents years ago and her parents, Jed and Grace, continued the upkeep of the old two-story house after her grandparents passed on. There were two bedrooms downstairs and two upstairs. Both Grace and Mary preferred the bedrooms downstairs and left the upstairs for guests. Not that they had many. Eventually other rooms upstairs took up storage. As she drove to the outskirts of Boone County, where flat land went on endlessly, she recalled Grandma Bryant's warmth and Grandpa Bryant's loud laughter.

Mary's home on these five acres of land took on a different perspective now.

Since her return home, she saw beauty in

the floors of the impressive old structure with their high-polished glow that her grandfather insisted on when the house was built. She treasured the oriental rugs, in spite of their faded corners and the ancient overstuffed furniture. She chuckled, as the window wipers of the car swished back and forth over the start of rain, thinking about her feelings as a teenager. The antique furniture and old rugs embarrassed her when friends visited. But not now! Her mother kept them looking their ultimate best. And most of all, her favorite old willow tree in the backyard, standing tall and firm, still bends occasionally to hear her most inner thoughts and secrets.

She'd been talking to the willow tree since six or seven years old. She'd sprawl out under that old tree and sometimes closed her eyes and mentally talk to her friend. Other times, she'd sit cross-legged with Winifred, her pet kitten, reading to both tree and cat.

Grace said, "I remember when Grandpa Bryant planted that tree, and Grandma came storming out the kitchen door shouting, 'Be sure you plant that tree right in the middle of the yard so it'll shade the kitchen window. I don't want that hot sun beating down on the house while I'm trying to cook.' And you can be sure he'd do exactly what she wanted."

The rain turned out to be a heavy shower, but a bright sun followed. Mary hoped that everything would dry outdoors later so she and her mother could relax on the cushioned white wicker chairs under the willow tree.

As she pulled onto the long gravel driveway and turned off the ignition, she looked around at the vast amount of land. She could see the sage bushes and large vegetable garden squared off and fenced at the back of the yard. All Grace's work! Her many long hours spent planting and nourishing large selections of vegetables and herbs now glowed with drops of rain. The breathless array of annuals and perennials that swayed in the breeze along the back and side of the yard were unbelievable. Neighbors and friends commented constantly on their beauty. What a shame that the winters of Illinois would hide them.

Mary checked the mailbox; nothing interesting there, just junk mail. Winifred's replacement Sissy, sat on the porch swing. Mary was amazed how much she resembled her mother who passed away a few years ago. As Mary opened the front door, a wonderful aroma greeted her. Sissy jumped off the swing and followed on her heels.

Grace yelled from the kitchen "Hi Mary, I'm doing a new recipe."

"Whatever it is, Mother, it sure smells good. I want to get into something more comfortable and I'll be right there. Do we have time for a glass of wine?"

"Absolutely, maybe even two."

Mary strolled back to the bedroom at the end of the long hall, and changed into her favorite jeans and blue cotton sweater. For some ungodly reason, Peter came into her mind. She left the comfortable old house three years ago at twenty-one to marry Peter Clark, a competitor's top journalist. The marriage lasted one year, and she returned home, thinking of him as one of the biggest mistakes of her life. *The single life for me,* she thought while pulling her hair back into a ponytail.

When she entered the kitchen, she found her mother with a bottle of olive oil in one hand and red wine vinegar in the other. She placed her arm around her mother's shoulder and gave her a squeeze.

"Okay, mother, what's the big surprise?"

"Well, I found this delicious-sounding recipe in the paper and I decided to try it.

It's a ground turkey spaghetti sauce with lots of herbs and spices. And to think I was able to get most of the herbs from my garden. That made me happy, Mary. We'll have a large vinaigrette salad and garlic bread to go with it. Doesn't that sound great?"

"It sure does."

Grace set the olive oil and vinegar down

on the counter. Opening the refrigerator door, she reached in and pulled out a chilled bottle of Zinfandel and two stem glasses.

"I think the April rain is gone and we can sit out under the tree now. Since it's such a nice day out there, let's give it a try. Grab the cushions on the porch, Mary."

Mary followed Grace out. When they approached the chairs, she noticed something new had been added. A round wrought iron end table with a glass top sat between the two chairs. Grace had placed a vase full of zinnias in the center.

"You've been shopping, Mother."

"Yes, I especially liked that it's painted white to match the chairs," Grace answered as she poured two stem glasses of wine.

After a bit of a silence between them, Grace spoke. "You know, Mary, Dad died six years ago today. I hate bringing up a sad subject, but it's been on my mind all day. Do you think we could go to Greenwood Cemetery tomorrow?

"It's Saturday and if the weather holds out, I'm sure we can."

"We are due to visit, dear. It's been some months since we've been there. I saw an article last week in the newspaper about new rules concerning the graves. It seems the cemetery prefers to take care of the graves and has asked family and friends to discontinue bringing flowers. They especially object to plastic flowers. When we get there, let's go over to the office and see if this is Greenwood's request also."

"Okay, Mother, let's check that out."

When Grace rose to check the dinner, Mary said, "Bring a couple of sweaters out, Mother. Don't you think it's a bit cool?"

While Grace went about her mission, Mary's thoughts drifted as she sat twirling her glass of wine. She would never forget her father's years of suffering, a no-nonsense type of guy who wore his worries on his sleeve. As an engineer with an aircraft corporation for many years, she remembered his job had a lot of responsibility and many nights he came home with severe headaches.

"These are stress headaches, Jed," Dr. Hughes said. "You worry too much. I'm going to give you some medication. But you have to learn how to relax."

He put up with the pain until he began to lose his eyesight. What came on gradually, developed into blindness. At the final diagnosis after many tests, Dr. Hughes said, "It a brain tumor, Jed. It's pressing in an area where surgery could be damaging and you would remain a vegetable."

He refused to stay in the hospital and his stubborn nature also refused to believe the seriousness of the diagnosis. Because he had good days and bad, he reminded Grace repeatedly that he would be fine with time.

Two months later, Jed lost sight of the first step of the staircase and tumbled down to the foyer. He was rushed to the hospital in an unconscious state and remained that way for weeks.

"I can't see him suffer anymore," Grace said. "Pray with me, Mary."

They knelt down under the large wall crucifix hanging in the master bedroom. The next morning, Jed took his last breath.

Tears filled Mary's eyes. She recalled that he died just before her divorce. After the funeral, she moved back home. A failed marriage and a heavy heart made her all the more determined never to leave again.

Within minutes, Grace returned with two sweaters on her arm and sat again. Mary leaned forward and said, "I applied for a new position today, Mother."

"Oh, are you unhappy where you are?"

Mary smiled. *Mothers always think you're unhappy when you make changes.*

"No, I'm not unhappy at all in the pool. The opportunity presented itself, and I thought it might be a good time to move on."

She explained about Liz Turner relocating to another state, but felt it was just too soon to say anything about Reed Lowell. The rain returned to the backyard. Mary lifted the cushions from the chairs as she and Grace made a mad dash for the back door.

* * *

Reed left the office at six o'clock, which was quite unusual for him. He normally stayed much later. Susie reminded him that there were two applicants for the Life and Arts position and he called back over his shoulder, "Leave those for morning."

He generally parked his black BMW in the back of the building. He strolled to his car, unlocked it and climbed in. He loved this car, especially the cream-colored leather interior, completely equipped with a car phone, and a small wet bar he specially had installed in the back seat for favorite clients. As he drove to Sally's florist on 5th Avenue, he felt important and he loved to feel important. Fifteen minutes later, he left the florist shop with a dozen red roses, jumped into his car and headed for Charles Street.

The huge wrought iron gate around the Cunningham mansion, usually locked for security reasons, needed to be activated by a voice box located on a post next to the driver's side of the car. Within minutes, Reed heard, "Yes, who is it, please."

He leaned a bit out of the car and said, "Reed Lowell." The gate swung open, exposing the long curved driveway, gorgeous green carpet grass, and huge budding oak trees, embraced with the backdrop of a sprawling four-story house. The whole setting should be captured on canvas, thought Reed.

As he approached the house, two gardeners were putting peat moss around the bushes and preparing the grounds for the on-coming summer. After the long winters in Illinois, the arrival of May begins to lift spirits and everyone becomes eager to plant an array of impatiens, petunias, snapdragons or any annual with color.

Reed drove the car to the end of the driveway, parked by the side of the house and jumped out. Taking two stairs at a time, he ran across the front porch and rang the doorbell. Victor, the house butler, opened the door and immediately said,

"Good afternoon, Mr. Lowell."

Reed smiled and said, "Hello, Victor. Where is Miss Cunningham?"

She's on the patio, Sir, having tea."

When Cheryl saw Reed coming through the patio doors, a pleased look crossed her face, and she smiled. "Hi, you're right on time."

He handed her the roses and bent over to kiss her. Cheryl gave him a light peck on the lips and walked over to an empty vase. Tara, the kitchen maid, came out and Cheryl handed her the flowers and vase. "Put these in water, Tara."

Reed looked at her for a couple of seconds and then said, "Well, that was short and sweet."

"What was?"

"That bird peck you gave me," Reed said grudgingly.

She didn't answer right away and after a few moments said, "Do you think we can spend one evening together without arguing? We have a wedding to plan and places to go. Let's do it without conflicts."

Reed decided to let it go. "Where are we going?"

"To see Pastor Laflin at Christ Lutheran Church on Park Avenue."

"We haven't selected a wedding date yet."

Cheryl studied him a minute and said, "I have."

"You mean you'd set a wedding date without consulting me?"

No two ways about it, he was annoyed.

"Let's not take this any further, Reed. We have a seven o'clock appointment, and it's a good half hour ride." He followed her into the house and out the front door with an angry frown. Suddenly, he was eight years old.

This is what tees me off, thought Reed. *This take-charge attitude she has. I can't let her get away with this.*

The time with Pastor Laflin went fairly well. Cheryl documented the wedding date on her calendar for Saturday, September 8th, at four o'clock in the afternoon. Reed accepted the date, but was tempted to nullify it.

Cheryl and Reed then tackled the next item on the list, reserving the ballroom at the Hilton Hotel. Cheryl informed the wedding coordinator that she not only wanted the huge ballroom, but the Court Garden. When the French doors of the ballroom were opened, guests could flow through the doors into the garden where a flowered arch would lead to a beautiful gazebo, covered with more flowers. Reed was stunned, not ever hearing this plan before. Never at any point in the conversation with the coordinator did she turn and ask Reed what he thought about the arrangement. Reed had a business mind and needed to hear the details of any and all arrangements made that involved him. Now, he began to show anger.

When Reed slammed the car door, Cheryl flinched.

"Ok, Cheryl, what was that all about?

"What, Reed?"

"Would it have hurt to tell me your plans before presenting it to the coordinator? I had no idea what you wanted. I refuse to stand around like a dunce while you run the show."

"You're always so busy, Reed. I know what I want with this wedding. Why should I discuss each detail with you when I can take charge and get it done! Cheryl became indignant. "Besides, the Cunningham's are paying the bills, so why should you care."

Reed caught the implication in her tone. *Did she mean the Cunningham's could always give her what she wanted even after they were married? This isn't the first time he's had misgivings about this marriage.* When he drove up to the front of the Cunningham's house, Cheryl leaned over to kiss him goodbye. He took the kiss on his cheek.

He always had a fitful night of sleep after a stormy evening with Cheryl, and tonight wasn't any different. He woke in the morning feeling miserable, like he had a heavy hangover. After a shower and a cup of coffee, he began to perk up a bit and decided the day would get better when he got to work. He walked into the newspaper office at nine o'clock with a cup of coffee in one hand and his briefcase in the other. This was much later than he normally arrived. Susie, typing at her desk, again reminded him of the applicants for the Life & Arts position.

Rubbing his brow, Reed asked, "Who are they, Susie?"

"One is Carol Langley from 'Movies and Stars,' and the other is Mary Bryant Clark, one of our best pool journalists."

"Have you got background reports on each?"

Susie brought forth two files and said, "Yes Sir. They're right here."

Reed took the files and started for his office. Hesitating for a moment, he turned and said to Susie,

"Let me look these over and I'll buzz you when I'm finished."

* * *

After a quick phone call the next morning and several apologies from Cheryl, Mary jumped right into developing an outline to follow while interviewing her on Friday. She decided to make a list of questions so as not to forget anything. Thinking about her own wedding to Peter Clark, she prepared her questions accordingly: Where, When, What time and How Many were the headings she placed across the top of her notebook page. She also sectioned off a place for names of the immediate family, close friends and wedding party.

As she became deeply involved in her assignment, the phone rang. She leaned over, picked up the receiver and said, "Yes, Mary here."

"Mary, this is Susie, Reed would like to

interview you this morning at eleven o'clock for the Life & Arts position. "Will you be available?"

Mary's heart raced as she glanced quickly at her desk calendar, saw nothing down for that time, and answered, "That will be fine, Susie."

"Good, see you then."

Thirty minutes before her appointment with Reed Lowell, Mary called home. Grace answered in her usual cheerful voice.

"Hello."

"Hi, Mother, just wanted to tell you I am going into Reed Lowell's office for an interview shortly."

"Oh, good luck dear. Now, don't be nervous; you have a lot to offer and will certainly be an asset to the company."

Mary had to admit she was a bit nervous about this interview. *What if he should ask me about the assignment I'm working on right now? How can I tell him I'm working on HIS wedding? Who knew he was marrying Cheryl Cunningham? Here I was beginning to zero in on the guy. Well, here goes nothing! Let the chips fall where they may.*

After letting all that run through her mind, Mary opened the door to Reed's office and walked in.

Susie was working at the file cabinet and turned around after hearing the door open.

"Hi, Mary. Take a seat for a minute. I'll let Reed know you're here."

Smiling, Mary picked up a nearby magazine and sat down. Her eye caught the article on diet and exercise, two subjects uppermost in her mind. She finished the article just as Susie motioned that Reed would see her now. He smiled when she walked into his office and extended his hand. "Please sit down, Mary." She felt his eyes on her as she leaned over to shake his hand.

"You don't mind if I call you Mary, do you?"

"Not at all, Mr. Lowell."

"Oh, please, call me Reed. Everybody does. I read the answer on the application regarding your reason for wanting the Life and Arts position, and I must say I'm impressed." Reed then got down to business and the rest of the interview went well. He assured her he would make his decision in a couple of days. But before she left his office, he asked, "Mary, how's Peter? I haven't seen him in a long time."

Mary was caught short on the question and hesitated before answering.

She blushed slightly and then said, "We were divorced six years ago."

"Oh, I didn't know. I only asked because he was a casual friend of mine and, in fact Mary, I attended your wedding, but only for a short while. I was unable to stay for the reception. Please forgive me for staring when you first came in, but I knew I had seen you before."

She just smiled. *No need to answer,* she thought, and returned to her office.

Mary couldn't help thinking about Reed Lowell as she drove home after work.

She began to talk out loud to herself. "If he attended my wedding, how is it I don't remember meeting him? He's attractive and very impressive. Something tells me, Peter didn't bother to introduce him. Not surprised at that. It sounds just like him!"

Mary found Grace sitting in the study with Sissy on her lap. Leftovers of the spaghetti sauce were simmering in the kitchen and Grace had her nose in a good book.

Mary kicked off her shoes in the corner of the room and Grace looked up.

"Well, Mary, how did the interview go?"

Mary hesitated at first, "I think well, Mother. Reed Lowell is a great guy. You know, he surprised me by saying he attended my wedding. I don't remember meeting him."

Grace leaned forward, "At your wedding, six years ago, and he remembered you?"

"Yes, he said Peter invited him, but he didn't stay long. I don't think Peter bothered to introduce him to me. That really sounds like something he could do."

"Well, Mary, that's neither here nor there. Do you think your chances are good for the position? Tell you what, before you answer that, I better check our dinner. I'll be right back." Grace rose from the chair, and Sissy jumped off. She followed Grace and the smell of food.

While Grace was gone, Mary sat in an overstuffed chair and savored the comfort of her surroundings. She loved this old house and the memories it held. If only it could speak. It would tell the world about Michael. The excitement he brought with him when Grace carried him home from the hospital. How, at ten years old, she let me hold him. *I'll never forget his strong hold on my little finger.*

She thought about her dad. How he told everyone he met about his son. A tear filled her eyes, remembering the shock when the doctor said, "He has a weak heart." This literally tore her father apart. Michael's death, at two years old, silenced her mother for a long time and changed her father completely. Mary often thought it may have contributed to his brain tumor.

When Grace returned from the kitchen, she found Mary staring out the back window where the spring flowers Grace planted all along the border near the fence glowed in a splendor of color.

"The backyard is beautiful, Mother. You've done a splendid job."

"Thank you, dear. Now, tell me do you think you'll get the job?"

"Yes, I do."

After dinner, Grace found peace and contentment in her book while Mary cleaned the kitchen. She sipped the remains of her wine, and let her thoughts settle on the interview with Reed, grateful he didn't ask about her current assignment. She wanted to speak with Cheryl Cunningham first before Reed discovered she had been assigned the interview.

Three

*R*eed decided to work overtime and forgot about calling Cheryl. It was seven o'clock when his phone rang. "Reed Lowell, here."

"Hi, darling" said Cheryl. "I took the liberty of setting up an appointment for Thursday to take care of other incidentals for the wedding. Is that okay with you?"

Reed cringed, "What incidentals?"

"Like the flowers and the wedding cake. We also need to discuss bridesmaids and groomsmen."

Reed decided no. There would be no more running around while she did all the talking and he stood like a big dope. "You know what you want for this wedding, Cheryl. I suggest you handle it yourself. I will take care of the groomsmen and tuxedos and you take care of the rest. I have a lot of work to do here and can't afford the time."

Suddenly, a different Cheryl appeared. "But, we should do these things together, Reed."

He softened. "Okay, you take care of the cake and flowers. I don't really know too much about those items anyway. Then, we can go out to dinner Friday night and discuss the bridesmaids and groomsmen. I'm certain who I want to stand with me and you can tell me who you have in mind. Is that all right with you?"

"That will be wonderful, darling. Goodnight for now."

Reed rubbed his eyes, put his paperwork away in the top drawer and decided to call it a night. On the way home, for no reason he could explain, he thought about Mary.

She certainly is a beauty, there's no doubt about that. It's not just that though. There's something about her that makes me want to know her better.

* * *

Mary awoke the following morning feeling fresh and energetic. She slipped into her car at eight fifteen with a determination to be completely organized before she met with Cheryl Cunningham.

Patty was typing diligently when she entered. She lifted her eyes to Mary and said, "Morning, Mary. You have a message on your desk that came in early this morning."

Mary stopped in front of Patty's desk and said, "Who's it from."

Patty frowned a bit and said, "I didn't recognize the name."

The note said, "It's urgent that I talk to you. Please call." At the bottom of the message, the name Helen Randall appeared and a telephone number. Mary looked at her watch. It indicated a little before nine. She decided to call. Mary knew Helen Randall well. Actually, she was Helen Clark Randall, Peter's mother. While married to Peter, Mary learned a lot about her. She led quite an affluent life with David Clark after they graduated from college. He rose quickly to administrative level in the Northern Illinois Gas Company, while Helen began her career in Interior Decorating. When she had her first child, Dave was already Vice President of the Company.

Oh, how well, I know Helen Randall, she thought. She remembered Helen's waste and selfishness. How she defended Peter's all-night parties and heavy drinking. It was okay with Helen when Peter would take off with the guys to ski over a weekend. What was it she'd say, "Being married doesn't mean he has to give up his friends, does it?" *She never found fault with his lifestyle, and I was just a nag. She stopped talking to me all these years after Peter and I divorced. Can't imagine what she wants now.*

Mary sat at her desk remembering even more; Dave Clark's massive heart attack and death in the obituary column of the newspaper, and Helen Clark's marriage to

Carl Randall two years later. Carl was an old friend of the family from their college days.

Word was spread through the grapevine that Helen's second marriage was for more money. Even though she had quite a bit of her own, she couldn't turn down Carl Randall, president of a successful appliance company. *Yes indeed, Mary knew Helen Randall.* Mary dialed the number and waited for an answer.

"Hello!"

Mary took a deep breath. "This is Mary, Helen. How are you?" Helen Randall's voice cracked and uncontrollable sobs began. "I wanted to be the one to tell you, Mary. Peter was killed yesterday skiing." She sobbed uncontrollably. Mary could barely make out what she was saying. "He lost control and plunged into a tree. He died of a broken neck. Oh, Mary, this is so awful."

She was dumbfounded and silent for a long moment. Helen finally said, "Mary, are you there? Did you hear me?"

The message took Mary's breath away. "Yes, I heard you."

Helen's voice became clearer as she said, "Would you come over, Mary? I know you and Peter were divorced, but I would love to see you and somehow I feel I could handle this if you were here. Please, Mary."

"No, no I don't want to know this and I

don't know how to handle this myself. How can I help you?" pounded in her head. Instead she replied, "I'll be right there, Helen."

Since Patty wasn't at her desk, Mary leaned over and wrote a note saying she'd be back in an hour. Something important came up.

* * *

As Mary pulled into the driveway on Roxbury Lane, she was flooded with memories. She could remember some good times in this house; times when she and her parents had elegantly prepared dinners in the main dining room, but she also remembered bad times when she and Peter fought. She decided not call Grace to tell her about Peter's death. She wanted to tell her in person that evening when she got home.

She rang the doorbell and to her surprise, Helen answered. Rose, Helen's housekeeper for years had always answered the doorbell.

"Hello, Mary."

Helen Randall, tiny, with a slight hump developing on the back of her neck from age, and osteoporosis, tilted her white, curly head. Mary could see that she was taking Peter's death very hard. Her eyes were puffy and red, but the deep blue still came through the puffiness. She always had a pretty face.

"Hello, Helen." They embraced. Then, Helen led Mary into the parlor off the foyer.

"Please sit down, Mary, and I'll ring for some tea."

When Rose came into the parlor, Mary smiled. She was grayer than when Mary last saw her, but still attractive. She remembered Rose, always calm and attentive with a capacity for calming others, being the only sane part of her life while married to Peter. Mary enjoyed the time she spent with her. She was more than a servant in this household. She was family.

"Bring some tea and cookies, Rose."

Rose turned to leave but hesitated when she saw Mary. "Oh, Mary, how nice to see you, it's been such a long time."

Mary still smiling, said, "Hello, Rose. It's very nice to see you, too!"

It was obvious that Helen delayed conversation while Rose served tea. She talked about numerous other subjects; the weather, work to be done on the house and even took Mary to see her array of roses on the patio. She was stalling so that Rose would not hear any of their conversation.

The second Rose walked out and closed the door, Helen's behavior changed. She pulled her handkerchief from her pocket and began to cry. "Mary, this is a terrible tragedy. I can't believe my Peter is gone. Will you be with me through this?"

Mary heaved a deep sigh. "You will have Karen and your family supporting you. And of course, there is Carl who will surely be a comfort to you through this whole ordeal."

Helen leaned over and touched Mary's hand, and tearfully said, "No one knew Peter like you Mary, not even his sister. He would want you there. He never stopped loving you."

Mary, still bitter about Peter, mused he sure had a lousy way of showing it.

"I'll do this for you, Helen. I know this appears harsh, but even under these circumstances, Peter's kind of hurt takes a long time to get over. I will not be a hypocrite and pretend I am doing it for him. What time is the memorial service?"

Helen rubbed her hands nervously together and answered, "Karen has set it up for eleven o'clock Friday morning at Sundberg's Funeral Home on Sixth Street."

Helen paused for a second then said, 'We learned through our lawyer, Mary, that you are mentioned in Peter's will. He has left some special items for you."

Mary decided not to ask what. "I have to go, Helen. I have an appointment. I will be here around ten thirty, Friday morning."

Opening the front door to exit, Mary avoided Helen's usual hug.

Instead of going back to the office, Mary went home. She opened the front door and steadied herself against the wall as she began to sob convulsively. Grace was in the kitchen, heard the violent sobbing, and ran into the foyer. She grabbed Mary and put her arms around her.

"Mary, what is it? Please, tell me what's wrong."

Finally, Mary controlled herself and sat down at the bottom of the staircase. "Mother, I'm sorry, I just had to let all of this anxiety out." She took a deep breath. "Peter Clark was killed skiing yesterday. I just came from Helen Randall's home. She called and insisted I come over...because she was distraught and claimed she needed me. This is all so terrible. I really want no part of it. Peter's death is not going to change the hurt in my heart no matter how much she begs. She insisted Peter would want me to be there with the family."

Grace was stunned. "Did you tell her you would be there with the family?"

Mary put her head down and quietly said, "Yes."

Grace could not hide her anger. "This is utter nonsense. She had no right to ask you that. You and Peter were divorced. If you wanted to go to the service, that should have been your decision not hers. Where's the service?"

"At Sundberg's Funeral Home, Friday morning."

"Then," Mary began, "she waved a carrot in my face by saying Peter made out a will and left me some special items. I don't want anything of Peter Clark's. I couldn't answer her on that. It turned my stomach."

Grace's heart felt heavy in her chest. "You are not under any obligation to sit with the family at that memorial service. You and I will go to the service, but we will sit where we want." Grace was defiant. Mary leaned on her for strength.

"But Mother, I told her I would be at the house Friday morning at ten thirty. The service is at eleven o'clock."

"Well, you just call, ask for Rose, and tell her something has come up and you will see the family at Sundberg's at eleven o'clock for the service. Rose will deliver the message for you. They will just get over it."

In spite of her trembling, Mary had to smile at her Mother's independence.

When Grace went back to the kitchen, Mary called the Randall household, hoping Rose would answer the phone. She did. Her apology was extended. She would not be able to sit with the Randall's on Friday morning.

She and Grace arrived at the funeral home at eleven o'clock on the dot. A directory was posted in the foyer of the funeral home announcing that a luncheon would be served at the home of Mr. and Mrs. Carl Randall's, after the service. Mary brought it to Grace's attention and Grace shook her head no. The decision was made.

To the left of the doors leading into the parlor were a row of empty chairs. She guided Grace quietly into two of the chairs, quite unnoticeably, since all faced the front of the parlor, where an array of beautiful flowers and wreaths were on display. In the center of the display was an elaborate mahogany urn which contained Peter's ashes.

After a short eulogy by Rev. Joseph Macdonald, members of the family and two of Peter's closest friends gave inspirational sayings and eulogies about their memories of Peter, some cried, some just sat somber. Mary noticed that Helen Randall sobbed quietly at times, but mainly was composed.

Mary knew it would be difficult to express condolences to Helen and her family since she backed off from being a part of the family presentation, but she wanted to cut off any relationship she had with these people and it was best to do it now. As she and Grace walked up to Helen and Carl, she could feel the frigid reception coming her way. The interchange was cordial, but mostly to Grace. Helen did not smile and Karen, Peter's sister, turned and walked away, refusing to even talk to her. Grace and Mary left.

Tuesday of the following week, a letter came from Peter's lawyer, Frank Knight, stating that articles of importance were left to her in his will and she was to contact him. She tried to think of what they might be, but to no avail, so she tucked the letter in her purse and decided to call from the office.

As she walked into her office, the phone rang. "Hello, Mary speaking."

"Mary, this is Susie. Wonder if you have an opening this afternoon at two o'clock? Reed would like to see you in his office."

With only a couple of phone calls to make, she said, "I'll be there."

She had worn her favorite chocolate brown suit this morning and Grace talked her into the multicolored bright scarf. Oh, how she hoped Reed had selected her for the Life & Arts position.

To get her mind off the excitement of everything, she placed her call to Peter's lawyer.

"Frank Knight speaking."

Mary cleared her throat and said, "Mr. Knight, this is Mary Bryant Clark. I received your letter regarding some articles that Peter left me in his will?"

His strong business-like voice answered, "Yes, Yes, Ms. Clark. I would rather not discuss this over the phone. Do you think you could come to my office one day this week?"

"It's a busy week, Mr. Knight, but I have some free time the following Monday morning about nine thirty. How would that be for you?"

"I think that will work, Ms. Clark."

As Mary got his address and suite number, she had a feeling any time would have worked for him.

After her conversation with Frank Knight, Mary placed a call to Cheryl Cunningham. Victor answered and put her through to Cheryl. "Cheryl, this is Mary Clark and I want to confirm our appointment for ten o'clock tomorrow morning."

Without hesitation, Cheryl said, "I'm so sorry, Miss Clark, I had to cancel our first appointment. Something very important came up. But I'm certainly looking forward to seeing you. Ten o'clock tomorrow is fine. If the weather continues to be as beautiful as it has been, would the patio garden be all right with you?"

"I'd love it out there, Cheryl. That would be great,"

As she hung up, Mary looked at her watch. She had hoped to run home for lunch but decided otherwise and went down to the company cafeteria for a salad. While waiting in line to pick up a salad, she looked around at the tables. Susie sat at one of the tables with someone familiar looking. As the "someone" turned her head to check the wall clock, Mary realized it was Peter's sister, Karen. Oh dear, she thought, if my name is mentioned, this could be disastrous.

Susie looked up, caught her eye and waved. Karen turned to see who she was waving to, and that did it. Mary knew her good name would be tarnished now. However, she was saved by a wave. Susie waved for her to come over. She picked up her salad and grabbed a coke and thought this was the thing to do to stop Karen from whispering in Susie's ear before she had her meeting with Reed Lowell. She remembered Karen's malicious behavior from the past.

"Hi, Karen!" said Mary. "I didn't realize you two knew one another."

Susie smiled. "Well, actually we met at a party a few months ago, and have become good friends."

Karen didn't speak or acknowledge Mary. After a few minutes of small talk, mainly between Susie and Mary, Karen stood up and said, "I have to go. I'll call you later, Susie. Good seeing you again Mary." With that, she was gone.

"Gosh," Susie said, "She sure was in a hurry."

Mary said, "Yeah, I wonder why!"

Susie checked her watch and said, "Oh, Mary, I better go too, it's one o'clock and I have some files to dig out for Reed. I'll see you shortly. Come down and have lunch with me some time soon."

Mary nodded and answered, "See you in an hour. Bye, Susie."

Four

*A*fter the brief lunch, Mary returned to her office. She opened her briefcase and went over her notes and the questions she had prepared for Cheryl Cunningham. Before she realized it, the clock on her desk read one forty-five. She combed her hair and brushed her face with a little powder. She returned her papers to the briefcase and headed for Reed's office.

Reed was at Susie's desk discussing some upcoming projects when Mary entered the suite of offices. He looked up and said, "Hi, Mary. Wait for me in my office and I'll be right with you." She sat in a big, comfortable leather chair set facing Reed's desk. He came in after a few minutes, smiling warmly. "How are you?"

"Just fine." She returned his smile.

Reed sat in his black leather chair and drew up closer to his desk.

"I've gone over your file, Mary, and I am impressed with your background. I've talked with Chuck Walton, your supervisor, as well as his associates, and they all assure me that you are doing a great job in the journalist pool. I understand you've been assigned to cover a wedding, but I never did hear whose getting married in our town."

Mary drew in a deep breath and said, "You."

He stared at her a minute and then simply said, "Me!"

Mary nodded and repeated, "You. Actually, the assignment said it was Cheryl Cunningham's wedding and I didn't find out you were the groom until I called Cheryl and set up an appointment."

Reed's crooked smile betrayed his surprise. Mary knew he was caught short. But he finally managed to say, "I'm sure you will do a great job, Mary."

To Mary's relief, he changed the subject quickly. "We finished our interviews, Mary, and have selected you for the Life and Arts position. There will be a three thousand dollar a year increase in your salary and then you will be evaluated after six months. How's that sound to you?"

Mary assured Reed that she would be satisfied with the increase and the evaluation, and thanked him for selecting her. She was bursting with excitement inside and couldn't wait to tell Grace.

Reed hesitated before continuing. "Liz Turner is leaving in two weeks, and I would like her to train you before she leaves. If we give the wedding assignment to someone else, then you could devote full time to Liz and the department, or do you have another suggestion?"

Mary pondered a few moments. "Reed, I am interviewing the bride tomorrow morning, and will have most of the information for the wedding at that time, except for a few incidentals when the day draws closer. We are approaching the beginning of May, and the wedding isn't until September, which should give me plenty of time to train and still do the illustrations and photography for the wedding. If you don't mind, I really would like to finish the job."

He immediately said, "I don't mind one bit, Mary. Since it's my wedding, I would be honored. Let me know if you have any problems. Incidentally, I am sorry about Peter's death. I just learned about it yesterday and would have attended the memorial service if I had known sooner."

Mary lowered her eyes and answered, "It was an unfortunate accident."

She extended her hand to Reed and as she turned to leave there was a tap at the door. Reed walked Mary out, and standing behind the huge walnut door was Phoebe, dressed in a black tailored pantsuit and yellow scarf. Her hair, always perfectly groomed, was pulled back into a French knot.

"Hi, Mother," Reed said. "Have you met

Mary?"

"Well, I was introduced to her on a formal basis when I toured the journalist pool, some time back, but would love to meet her on an informal basis."

"This is your opportunity to meet her on an informal basis. She's been selected for the Life & Arts position."

"That's great, Mary. Good luck to you in your new position." said Phoebe. "By the way, are you Jed and Grace's daughter?"

"Yes."

"We had met them at several holiday functions some years ago. The community experienced a great loss with your father's death."

Mary felt Phoebe's eyes studying her. She thanked her for her kind words about her father.

There was jubilation in the Bryant house, and Grace prepared another wonderful dinner. Her menu of a standing rib roast, browned potatoes, breaded cauliflower, butternut squash, salad and hot cornbread would get a standing ovation. And, of course, the willow tree would again be the scene of a toast to Mary for capturing the Life and Arts position.

The next morning Mary awoke jumped out of bed and flew into the bathroom. After a refreshing shower, grapefruit for breakfast and two cups of coffee, she bounded out of the house, set for a challenging day with Cheryl Cunningham. She arrived at ten o'clock on the dot and rang the doorbell. While she waited, she looked over the landscaping, flowers and beauty of the estate grounds.

The door opened and Victor said, "Yes, can I help you?"

"I'm Mary Bryant Clark and I have an appointment with Cheryl Cunningham at ten o'clock."

"Come in, Madam. I will tell her you are here."

As Mary took in the gold railing staircase with marble stairs, high-vaulted ceilings, gorgeous chandeliers and display of paintings and family portraits, she blew out a low whistle. Victor returned and led Mary to the garden patio where Cheryl was having tea, dressed in a flowing ankle-length dress with large red roses on a black background. Her long, blonde hair, pulled back from her face and clipped in the back, was very becoming. Mary felt she fit in perfectly with the beauty of the garden that surrounded her.

The patio was engulfed with azalea bushes, ripe for blooming. One had blossomed and the red was breathtaking. Mary held her breath, admiring the beauty of the setting. Mozart's music would have been more appropriate than discussing business.

Cheryl smiled, extended her hand and said, "Hello, Miss Clark. Please have a seat and some tea."

"Please call me Mary. Before we begin, I really have to comment on how beautiful your patio and yard are."

"Thank you, we have a wonderful group of people that keep it looking like this. Would you please call me Cheryl?"

As Cheryl poured tea, Mary said "Shall we begin?"

Cheryl nodded. Mary opened her briefcase and pulled out her prepared notes with a list of questions. Nearly three hours were spent getting every bit of information necessary about the wedding and Mary informed Cheryl that she would arrive on September 8th, the day of the wedding, to monitor her entire day from her last breakfast alone on the patio until the bride and groom left the reception. She assured Cheryl her efficient camera would be taking photographs constantly along the way. The whole affair would be printed as a full-page display in the "The Lowell Report." Mary saw a satisfied grin cross Cheryl's face. Yet, on the other hand, some small display of sadness in her eyes.

On her way back to the office, Mary stopped at a telephone booth to make a call to Patty.

"Hi, Patty," said Mary. "Do me a favor.

Check the company directory and give me Liz Turner's extension please."

After a few moments, Patty said, "Liz Turner's extension is 235.

"What's going on, Mary?"

Mary, smiling from ear to ear said, "Well, you are now talking to the new Director of the Life and Arts Department."

"You're kidding."

"Oh, I wouldn't kid about something like this. I can't believe it myself. Reed Lowell assigned me the job yesterday. Patty, I am very excited and want to start training with Liz as soon as possible."

Patty could only say, "I will miss you, Mary. You have been great to work with. But, congratulations, you deserve it."

Mary extended her thanks, and Patty switched her over to extension 235.

Mary glanced at her watch, one-fifteen. She hoped Liz would answer.

After three long rings. "Hello, Liz Turner."

"Liz, this is Mary Clark. I happened to be the lucky one who will replace you. You will be greatly missed and I hope to do as good a job as you have. Reed Lowell asked that I contact you. Perhaps, we could set up a time to get together?"

"What are you doing now, Mary? I have some free time this afternoon. We could go over a few details."

"I'm on my way back to the office and I could see you in about thirty minutes. Is that okay?"

"That's fine, Mary. I'll be here waiting for you."

Mary didn't want Liz waiting too long for her so she hurried to the office. She saw the traffic light turn green as she got to the intersection of East State Street and Arnold. Heading north and checking the traffic on her right, Mary didn't see the red Pontiac speeding through the intersection on her left before it slammed into the driver's side of her car, spun it around, and flipped it over.

Someone called an ambulance and the police. The left side of Mary's head was jammed between the door and the steering wheel. It seemed she was barely alive. Her legs were twisted in the opposite direction of her body. It took over an hour to remove her from the car. The paramedics strapped her on a gurney and rushed her to St. Anthony's Medical Center.

Five

Sam Petrello opened Mary's purse and looked for identification. Her wallet showed a driver's license, credit cards, insurance medical card and a card identifying her as an employee of *The Lowell Report*. Unable to get an answer at her home, Officer Petrello called the phone number on the company card. The main operator heard the urgency in the officer's voice, and put the call through to Reed Lowell.

Reed answered the phone. "Reed Lowell here,"

"Mr. Lowell, this is Officer Petrello of the Rockford Police Department. I'm at the scene of an accident where a Mary Bryant Clark has been seriously injured. According to the information found in her purse, she works for your newspaper. Is that right?"

Reed slumped down in his chair and stared. He was too stunned to utter a word.

"Mr. Lowell, are you there?"

A shiver ran throughout his entire body. Reed answered, "Yes, yes, Officer, I'm here."

"Mr. Lowell, we were unable to get

anyone on her home phone. If she has a family, they need to be notified."

Before Officer Petrello could say more, Reed quickly said, "She lives with her mother. I'll call her immediately."

* * *

Grace hummed a tune as she vacuumed. The phone rang several times. She caught the last ring, turned off the vacuum cleaner, and ran to the phone.

"Hello, hello," she answered quickly.

"This is Reed Lowell from *The Lowell Report.* Is this Mrs. Bryant?

"Yes, I am Grace Bryant."

"Mrs. Bryant, I would like to talk to you. May I come over now?"

"Is there anything wrong, Mr. Lowell?"

Reed ignored her question. "I need instructions to your home, Mrs. Bryant, and I'll be right over."

Twenty minutes later, Reed could see Grace watching from the front window as he pulled into the driveway. As he ran up the front stairs, she immediately opened the door.

"Come in," she said.

Reed glanced quickly around and followed Grace into the living room.

She motioned to a comfortable overstuffed chair. "Please sit down. Now,

Mr. Lowell, what is this all about?"

* * *

Reed and Grace rushed into St. Anthony's Medical Center only to discover that Mary had been switched to Rockford Memorial Hospital because of the severity of her injuries. They left immediately and drove quickly to the hospital. The receptionist at the admittance desk asked someone to take them to emergency at once.

Mary was in surgery. Nurse Albertson showed them the waiting room and said the doctor assigned to Mary, Dr. Gordon, would be in to see them as soon as she was out of surgery.

Reed walked the floor of the waiting room, while Grace sat and stared through blank eyes. He would glance at her every so often. She seemed in a state of shock. At one point, he stopped walking and asked if he could get her something to drink. She just shook her head no.

Reed finally sat down next to her, realizing they had a long wait. Grace reached over and touched his hand. "She was so happy. We had a little party last night to celebrate her new job," she sobbed. "She loves the willow tree. We sit under it every night and sip wine to relax. She especially liked the idea of being head of a department and reporting to you, Mr. Lowell. Why did this have to happen?" Grace dropped her face in her hands and sobbed bitterly. Reed put his arm around her and let her sob into his shoulder.

After an endless wait, Dr. Gordon, still wearing his surgical garments, came through the swinging hospital doors. Reed and Grace were the only two people in the waiting room. Reed stood up immediately and extended his hand. "I'm Reed Lowell and this is Mary's mother, Mrs. Bryant. How is Mary?"

Dr. Gordon looked over his half glasses and said, "There is extensive damage on the left temporal lobe of her brain. She has had a full body seizure and we have placed a breathing tube in her throat to make sure she is getting enough oxygen. Her prognosis is uncertain at this time, but we are doing everything we can. Her legs are also a major concern. They are severely twisted, but we cannot do anything about that right now. She is lucky to be alive."

Grace closed her eyes and sighed deeply after hearing the doctor's prognosis. With tears rolling down her cheeks, she asked, "Can we see her, Doctor?"

Dr. Gordon hesitated before saying, "She's in Intensive Care. I'll send Nurse Albertson in to take you there, but please don't stay long."

Reed and Grace stood mesmerized, looking down at the tubes and needles in Mary's body. Grace cried quietly as she touched Mary's face; the entire left side was bruised and marked with scratches. Her beautiful auburn hair had been shaved and her head was bandaged. Reed could see the impression of her legs under the covers, and cringed at how distorted they were. Yes, she was lucky to be alive, all right, he thought, but will she ever be normal again? Tears filled his eyes, for the impact of this tragedy was just too much

Finally, Reed took Grace's elbow and whispered, "We should leave now. I'll take you home." Grace turned to leave. Her body was slumped over and frail looking, as if she had aged drastically in a single moment.

They drove in silence and Reed walked Grace to her door. As she took out her key, he asked, "Are you going to be all right? Would you like someone to stay with you tonight?" Grace looked up at Reed, and with tear-filled eyes quietly said, "I have good neighbors, Mr. Lowell. If I need anyone I can call them. Thank you for staying with me through all of this." He hugged her and left.

Grace closed the door after Reed left and placed her hat and purse on the foyer table. She was numb from head to toe and held onto the table for a few moments, then slowly turned to enter the parlor. As she thumped into her favorite chair, her hands flew to her face and she sobbed deeply, causing tears to overflow down her hands and into her lap.

"Why, Lord, why? What were you thinking?

Grace knew the Lord well. She found him when Jed was suffering and then died with a brain tumor. While he slept, she'd drive a few blocks day after day to a nearby chapel. She'd light a candle and pray. After the funeral, she accepted the outcome, devoting her time and love to Mary. But now, darn it, this is asking too much.

She hammered the arm of the chair and shouted out until completely exhausted, then rose and staggered to her bedroom. Fully clothed, she fell across her bed and slept.

* * *

Reed drove back to the office blindly. Tears welled in the corner of his eyes causing stop lights to blur as he returned to the office. As Susie stared at him in disbelief, he asked her to call a meeting for all employees in the conference room. It was just short of quitting time, and most showed up. After the announcement about Mary, all were stunned and quiet. Patty left the room sobbing hysterically. Phoebe ran to calm her, and then asked Susie to call the florist and send a bouquet of flowers. Her final request was for all employees to pray.

The following morning, Reed woke up early. After showering and drinking his first cup of coffee, he called his mother. They discussed Mary's accident and Phoebe asked if there was anything she could do. "Not just now, Mother, but I may need you later." After his call to Phoebe, he dialed Grace's number.

"Mrs. Bryant, this is Reed Lowell. I was wondering if you needed a ride to the hospital today. I'm going to see Mary and would be glad to pick you up."

Reed could detect the weakness in Grace's voice when she answered and he wondered if she had slept at all the night before.

"Yes, Mr. Lowell, I intend to go. You are so kind to offer. What time are you going?"

"Call me Reed, please. I can't help thinking about Mary, and am anxious to talk to the doctor. Maybe, we can see her again. How would nine o'clock be for you?"

"I'll be ready when you arrive."

Again, Reed and Grace drove silently to Rockford Memorial Hospital. He pulled up in front of the hospital and turned to Grace saying, "Looks like a busy day, so I'm going to let you out here while I look for a parking place. You might want to ask if Mary is still in Intensive Care."

"I would rather wait for you, Reed. I'll be sitting in the lobby when you return."

Reed hesitated at first and then realized that Grace might need an arm to lean on before seeing Mary again. Her somber face worried him. Anxious thoughts ran through his mind as he pulled his BMW into a parking space right under the shade of a huge oak tree. The morning sun already signaled high temperatures.

As he walked to the front entrance of the hospital, he removed his suit jacket, opened his shirt collar and loosened his tie. Slipping into the revolving door, he caught sight of Grace sitting on a soft chair next to an artificial plant. She didn't acknowledge him. She simply stared into space.

To get her attention, he said "Well, there you are. Shall we go?"

Without a word, Grace accepted Reed's hand. They walked to the reception desk and asked if Mary was still in Intensive Care. Could they see her? After a few minutes, the silver elevator doors opened wide and they both stepped in. Reed pushed the button for the third floor and they remained silent as they ascended to the reason their life had changed so drastically. Reed could hear Grace's heavy breathing in the silence of the elevator.

Reed spotted Dr. Gordon coming down

the hall as they exited the elevator. The information area buzzed with ant-like activity; nurses and aides rushed around checking charts and answering phones. Dr. Gordon saw Reed's hand signal and stopped in front of the Intensive Care Unit. As they got closer to him, Grace rested her hand on Reed's arm for support.

"We wanted to see Mary, Doctor. Can you tell us where she's located?"

"She's been moved into Room 312. That's just down the hall. Are you a relative?"

As Grace released Reed's arm and walked down the hall to see Mary, Reed thought this a good opportunity to talk to the doctor privately.

"No, doctor, I'm not a relative. Mary is an employee at my company. She lives with her mother, who is so distraught over her condition that I'm trying to protect her from hearing the worst of this situation. Do you mind if we talk privately for a few minutes? I want to help. I'm looking for some answers."

Dr. Gordon removed his glasses saying, "Of course, Mr. Lowell, I understand your concern for Mary's mother, but under the circumstances she will have to be present before I can go into detail about Mary's condition. You can be present, but a family member must be part of the consultation."

"Can I take a moment to get Grace now? Have you got the time?"

"Yes, if you make haste." Dr. Gordon smiled.

Reed and Grace were led into a small conference room to the left of the elevators. Dr. Gordon pulled out one of the conference table chairs for Grace and motioned for her to sit. He rolled out the head chair for himself and sat next to Reed. He replaced his glasses and removed a small pad and pen from the breast pocket of his white coat.

He sketched a drawing of Mary's brain, turned to both of them, but directed his attention to Grace.

"There's a report on her this morning. Most of the damage is on the left side of the brain where Mary's head hit the steering wheel after the impact. Therefore, her memory could be affected. There is a great deal of swelling in this area and we need time to allow it to decrease. Before we do any extensive surgery, I feel it's best to let nature takes its course to repair the affected area slowly. We know from the several x-rays we've taken that her injuries are self-contained in that particular area and time will tell if her speaking, hearing or personality will change in any way."

Dr. Gordon removed his glasses and laid them on the table before continuing. "Actually, I am more concerned about

Mary's legs. We may have to do more than one surgery to straighten them. The right leg is injured more than the left. Bone replacement and skin grafting might be necessary. Then, there will be months of physical therapy. This is a very slow process and all very overwhelming to you now, but don't get discouraged. Most of it depends on Mary's willingness to work hard on improving."

Both Reed and Grace listened carefully to every word. After a moment, Grace asked, "When will she come out of this coma stage she's in?"

"Hard to say! I would guess in about a week, we could see a different Mary, but don't hold me to that."

Reed decided to jump in with a question. "What does that mean?"

"She should start opening her eyes and hearing people talk to her. The decline in swelling will make a tremendous difference. But, there are twists we have to worry about - psychological twists."

Grace hesitated at first, "I...in what way?"

"If Mary's concentration or memory are diminished in any way, she can become anxious or depressed - psychological conditions that exacerbate the physical problem. The brain does try to heal itself while going through rehabilitation, but each person progresses at a different pace. We must keep her from becoming anxious or depressed because the healing process is taking longer than she expects."

At that, Dr. Gordon rose, shook hands with Reed and departed with a smile. As Reed and Grace walked to the Intensive Care ward to see Mary, he felt the trembling going through Grace's body as she took his arm to steady herself.

Six

*C*heryl Cunningham read the newspaper report on Mary two days later, and called Reed. He told her he would send someone else out to handle the wedding story. He had not decided who yet.

"There's time, Cheryl. Let me think about it."

With so much to do at the newspaper, he wondered why he continued to remain involved in Mary's accident. Her diligence as a responsible employee surely deserved compassion and recognition, but driving back and forth to the hospital every day? Really now, was that necessary? The whole incident began to take a toll on him.

The following morning, to keep the business running properly, he decided to assign Carol Langley to the Life and Arts position. Liz Turner had a week left before leaving the newspaper and he thought that would be enough time to train Carol. But he had to get someone to take Grace to the hospital since she didn't drive. He hesitated to call, but then made his decision.

"Grace, this is Reed. I have a number of

meetings and traveling assignments planned so I've arranged for one of our office boys to pick you up and drive you to the hospital every day. His name is Jimmy Allen, and he's very responsible. I've given him your phone number. He'll call you sometime today. I hope that's all right with you."

At first, Reed heard only her breathing. Then she said, "That's fine. Thanks for letting me know."

However, he felt guilty about deserting her. From time to time, as he drove past the hospital, he'd stop to check on Mary. She was always the same. He longed desperately for a change. But, each time he visited, she remained the same. Her head wrapped in bandages, her body sprawled in the bed, eyes closed, completely comatose, with no sign of change. He even began to feel responsible for the accident. He didn't know why.

When talking to Phoebe, he tried to act calm, but his anxiety about Mary began to surface and Phoebe noticed the change in him.

"Reed, Mary's accident isn't your fault. Susie and I were discussing her condition and we both agree you're getting too involved. Your wedding is right around the corner. Cheryl called me last night. She said you had planned a date to discuss the bridesmaids and groomsmen and you cancelled. What's going on with you anyway?"

Reed walked away from his desk and looked out the window. "I don't know, Mother. At times, I think it's Grace. She is suffering so over this. And at other times...I just feel compelled to help. Each time I see Mary in her comatose state, her legs in splints under the covers, my heart bleeds."

"I can understand your feelings, Reed. But, Cheryl means something to you also.

I feel you're shirking your responsibility to her. You're giving full attention to a young lady you don't even know."

"I want to know her though, Mother. For some ungodly reason, I want to know her!"

Phoebe shook her head, and left the room with a disgusted look on her face.

* * *

Weeks went by. Mary remained the same. IV bottles were changed, doctors did their routine checks on her, orders were given to wheel her to x-ray for more tests, and Nurse Appleton smiled as Grace came in. But Grace wasn't vocal with anyone except the young man who drove her back and forth, and that only amounted to "hello" and "goodbye."

One day, the kitchen wall phone rang as Grace opened the front door, after her neighbor had driven her to the grocery store. She placed her two bags of groceries on the table and rushed to the phone. It was Nurse Appleton from the hospital.

At the same time, Reed had about ten minutes between lunch and a client's appearance, scheduled for one thirty. Never a day went by that he didn't think of Mary and he decided to call Grace. When she answered the phone, Grace was ecstatic. Mary had opened her eyes.

"I'm so glad you called, Reed. Nurse Appleton just called to say, she's awake. Mary is awake."

Reed could hear the sobs in her voice as a shiver ran through his body.

"When did it happen?" he asked.

"Nurse Albertson said fifteen minutes ago. She thought I should come to the hospital."

"Let's go. I'll be right there."

Reed called Susie on his car phone. "Cancel my appointment with Mr. Carter, Susie. Tell him I'll call to set up another. I had an emergency…tell him anything."

The pair rushed from Grace's house, through traffic, into the parking lot, and up the hospital steps. The delayed elevator nearly drove them crazy and finally they rushed down the hall to Room 312. Nurse Appleton stood at Mary's bedside, massaging her arms. She looked up as they quietly came into the room.

"She only opened her eyes once, but she did smile. I think if you stay awhile, she may open them again," said Nurse Appleton.

Grace took Mary's hand and looked up at Reed. "She looks so serene and beautiful, doesn't she Reed?"

Reed stared at the form lying in the bed and said, "Yes, beautiful."

While Grace and Reed stared down at Mary, Dr. Gordon came into the room. "Well, we are encouraged," he said, placing a pen in his white coat pocket. "I understand from Nurse Appleton that Mary is slowly coming around. She had a scan this morning, and we can see that the swelling is beginning to decrease. That's a very good sign."

Grace breathed a deep sigh of relief, and Reed saw her lift Mary's hand to her heart.

"Her legs, however, are still a major concern; but we must take one step at a time. She has a long way to go, and there's certainly hope."

After Dr. Gordon left, Nurse Appleton asked Grace and Reed if they'd like a cup of coffee. Reed refused and Grace walked with the nurse down the hall to the lounge.

Alone with Mary now, Reed drew a chair to the side of the bed and held Mary's hand. He caught the smell of lilacs from the bouquet of flowers on the end table next to the bed. There were numerous cards from well-wishers and a framed picture of an older gentleman standing next to a willow tree. This must be Mary's father, he thought.

Turning his eyes to Mary, he could see the pink returning to her cheeks. Could she really come through this and why am I so concerned? Phoebe is right. I've only had a casual meeting with her once or twice. He wondered if Grace kept him coming. She was the kind of mother anybody would love to have. Phoebe was a good mother, too, but so business oriented. He remembered her being gone and involved in the newspaper most of the time when he was a boy growing up. She always had to be right there with his dad when big decisions were made.

Grace was gentle, caring, ready to listen and about as sweet as they come. He liked that. Somehow, he felt Mary could be like that, too. As he stroked her arm in deep thought, he heard a moan and turned his head. It was coming from Mary. He waited a bit and then he saw her head twist back and forth. When she opened her eyes, Reed smiled down at her.

"Hello, welcome back," he said. She stared wide-eyed for a few minutes, softened her expression, and then tears began to roll down her cheeks. Reed bent over, pushed a tear aside and without any hesitation, kissed Mary lightly on the lips. She closed her eyes, smiled and fell into a deep sleep.

As Reed straightened, Grace and a resident doctor entered the room. Reed's excitement caught hold of him and he blurted out, "Mary opened her eyes and smiled."

Grace hurried to the bedside.

The doctor checked Mary's pulse and said, "She should be coming around more and more as time goes on and, hopefully, she will remember who she is and who you are."

Reed looked down at Mary and said, "What can we do to help?"

"Stay with her through this and pray! She could have vision problems down the road, and she will need support through the leg surgeries. She's going to need strong support from those who love her."

Reed and Grace remained at the hospital until dinner time, hoping Mary would awake again. Since there was no sign of that happening, Nurse Appleton suggested the cafeteria on the first floor for some relatively good food.

After dropping Grace off, Reed headed for home. He thought about the doctor's comments as he drove, especially the part about Mary needing support from those who love her. LOVE HER!! Is that what this is about? Do I love her? How could I, he thought. I don't even know her. Why did I bend down and kiss her lips? I could have kissed her on the forehead. Why the lips? Because they were so inviting? Yes, they were.

By the time Reed pulled into his driveway, he was sweating heavily and trembling slightly. He opened the front door and hurried to the bathroom. He took a cold shower, jumped into his pajamas, thought about a night cap, but decided to go right to bed. He never gave calling Cheryl a second thought.

Seven

Frank Knight, Peter Clark's lawyer, sat in his office Monday morning waiting for Mary to arrive. At eleven o'clock, he became restless, reached for his intercom and buzzed his secretary.

"Yes, Mr. Knight,"

"Any word from Mary Clark?"

"No, I'm afraid not. Mr. Knight. I'll try her office."

After the third ring, Patty answered, "Miss Clark's phone. How can I help you?"

"This is Frank Knight's office calling. Miss Clark had an appointment with Mr. Knight this morning at ten thirty. We have no record of a cancellation. Can you tell us if she plans to keep her appointment?"

Patty remembered going through Mary's calendar canceling all of her appointments but she had missed this one.

"Please tell Mr. Knight that somehow I overlooked calling him to cancel this appointment. I'm so very sorry. Mary has been in a terrible car accident and is in Intensive Care at Rockford Memorial Hospital. We have not received a report on her for today, but you will hear from us when we are able to set up another appointment."

Knight's secretary passed the information on to him and he immediately called Helen Randall.

* * *

Helen Randall, dressed in her usual garden clothes; blue jeans, yellow smock and large straw hat, was pruning her bushes. She heard Rose answer the telephone through the open window of the office.

Rose called to her. "It's Frank Knight, Mrs. Randall. Do you want to take it?"

Helen nodded and hurried to the house. Removing her garden gloves, she picked up the receiver and said, "Hello Frank."

"Helen, I have some interesting information for you. I hadn't seen the morning papers lately, so perhaps you already know about Mary Clark."

"Know what?" Helen asked.

"She was in a terrible automobile accident and is in Intensive Care at Rockford Memorial Hospital."

Helen froze. "When did this happen?"

"A few days ago. I had an appointment set up with her to go over Peter's will, and she never showed. My secretary checked on her and found she was in the hospital. In pretty bad shape, I understand."

Helen remained silent for a few seconds, "Then she doesn't know about the brooch?"

"No," answered Frank, "or the watch."

Helen's voice was throaty and a slanderous look crossed her face.

"I don't give a damn about the watch, Frank. It's that valuable brooch I want back. If she doesn't know Peter willed it to her than just give it back to me. Give her the watch."

"It doesn't work that way, Helen. The will is a legal document and must be complied with until the statute of limitation runs out. Mary has her rights, too."

Helen cringed. "She has no right to that brooch. It has been in our family for years and Peter shouldn't have given it to her. I want it back, Frank, and I will get it."

Helen hung up.

* * *

Frank pulled open the bottom drawer of his desk and pulled out a manila envelope. He drew out two items wrapped in white tissue paper. He opened the larger item of the two. It was a man's Rolex watch with two diamonds on each side. On the back, Frank read, "To Peter with love, Mary."

After setting the watch aside, Frank opened the second article, and brought forth a dark green velvet drawstring bag. Pulling open the strings, Frank lifted the brooch from the bag. It was a heart-shaped mother of pearl cameo, surrounded with a row of twelve diamonds and a wide gold band. It was exquisite and, he assumed, worth a fortune. No wonder she wants it back. He put them back in the envelope and walked over to one of his bookcases. He located a safe behind one of the books. Dialing the code number, he opened the door, placed the items inside and locked the safe.

Frank Knight had taken over Paul Westerfield's law office after he retired a few years ago. Paul was a pricey lawyer who had several wealthy families as clients; one being Dave and Helen Clark. Frank Knight was a partner. Since the office was in the downtown area of Rockford, business was very good for Frank, but his methods were not always honorable. He stretched the law and created loopholes for a couple of clients. That got him into trouble which caused gossip and concern by some Rockford citizens. Two years ago, he lost an important case for an Express Company that he should have won, causing a great deal of speculation. Helen Clark kept Frank as her lawyer until she married Carl Randall. Peter, however, liked Frank Knight and retained him as his lawyer until his death.

* * *

Helen Randall returned to pruning and gathering roses after talking to Frank Knight but her mind was unsettled. She had become so obsessed with getting the brooch back that she decided to take matters into her own hands. Gathering up her garden tools, plopping them into a basket and removing her gloves, she walked into the garage. The roses would have to wait. She had something much more important to do.

It was eleven o'clock when she walked out the door dressed in a purple two-piece suit, highlighted with a floral scarf arranged around her neck. The outfit enhanced Helen's white hair, and complimented her pretty face. Rose caught sight of her and asked hurriedly, "Will you be back for lunch, Mrs. Randall?"

Pulling back, she looked up at the Grandfather Clock that stood in the foyer, and answered, "Plan it a little later, Rose. Ask Carl if he wouldn't mind having lunch around one or one-thirty. If he can't wait that long, then feed him. I'll grab a snack when I get home."

Rose accepted that and Helen closed the door, never mentioning where she was going.

Helen was chauffeured by Andy Carr for the past four or five years, ever since her close encounter with a speeding truck. Frightened beyond words, she vowed never to drive again.

As she approached the black, sleek Cadillac, he was already holding the door open for her, and saying, "Where to, Madam?"

Helen slid into the rich, leather back seat and said, "Rockford Memorial Hospital."

As her chauffer drove, Helen's thoughts raced back to memories of her first encounter with Mary. She remembered Peter's excitement as he swung her around on the back veranda. Something he enjoyed doing because she pretended annoyance.

"Put me down, Silly! What's wrong with you?"

"Oh Mother, I just met the most beautiful woman in the world."

"I have quit counting all the beautiful women you have met, Peter."

Peter Clark's blond hair and handsome face attracted women easily. He could have his pick, but his love for the high life and good times kept him single at thirty-one.

This time it was different.

Helen remembered the party he arranged, inviting all of his friends and family to meet Mary. No two ways about it, she was beautiful, but serious and disciplined, more so than Peter. That's okay, thought Helen. Actually, she liked Mary. Until she learned that Peter, without consulting her, gave Mary the gorgeous brooch for a wedding gift.

As the black Cadillac drove up to Memorial Hospital, a sneer crossed Helen's face as she remarked in a low voice, "I WILL get that brooch back."

Andy Carr opened the car door, and Helen made her way up the stairs. She stopped at the admittance desk, asked for Mary's room number and then turned left into the gift shop. There, in a corner next to book selections and greeting cards, was a flowering pink jasmine plant displayed in an attractive gold pot, priced at $69.98.

"I'll take it," she told the girl behind the counter. Have it sent up to Room 312." Upon leaving the gift shop, Helen entered into the elevator, pushed the third floor button and made her way to Mary's room.

In the meantime, Dr. Gordon was visiting Mary. He checked her vital signs and read her chart. As he worked, he noticed a smile on Mary's face.

He had hoped for a change in her condition since it had been two weeks since her accident. For some reason, he looked for it today as he walked into her room, and his wish had been granted. In spite of his surprise and delight, he decided to play along when he noticed the smile on Mary's face.

"It's about time you woke up?" he said in a joking voice.

Mary opened her eyes. Continuing to smile, she said, "I thought I'd fool you into thinking I was still comatose."

"How are you feeling?"

"I've been better, but glad to be alive. I'm worried about my legs, Doctor."

"Mary, you are responding wonderfully. Each case is different. We didn't know how you would come out of your delirium; whether you would know us, your family or even yourself. Now these fears are behind us and we can concentrate on your legs."

Mary was still taking strong drugs and could only listen or be attentive for a short time before falling off to sleep. Dr. Gordon noticed her eyelids getting heavy, so he just patted her hand and said, "We will talk about this again."

He lifted her chart hanging at the end of the bed and ordered x-rays of her legs for the afternoon. But as he turned to leave, he found a striking older woman in a purple suit standing in the doorway.

"She just dozed off. But come in, she is in and out of a sleep pattern and may want to see you."

As he passed Helen Randall, the aroma of her perfume pleased him. He closed the door and left Helen in the quiet of the sterile room. Helen eyed the room wondering where the pink jasmine plant would look its best. In searching, she noticed the lilacs in a large green-striped vase on a desk in the corner.

A tap at the door led her to open it just as Mary opened her eyes. The gift shop delivery boy stood holding the gold pot containing the flowering jasmine and Helen motioned him in. A table on the opposite side of the room adjacent to the lilacs caught Helen's eye and she pointed to the table. The boy placed it down and left.

The movement in the room was blurry to Mary. She heard a voice but couldn't identify it. Helen bent over and said, "Hello, Mary. How are you today?"

Mary recognized the voice and the whiff of perfume. Helen had worn the same perfume for years.

"Do you know who this is, Mary?"

Mary closed her eyes. Helen drew up a chair, took Mary's hand and sat down. She was startled to see Mary's bandaged head and contorted legs under the sheet, and quickly concluded that Mary would never be the same.

The door opened again. This time it was Nurse Albertson.

"Oh hello!" Since Mary's eyes were closed, she asked "Does Mary know you're here?"

"Her eyes opened for just a minute, but

now she's dozed off again."

Mary's eyes were closed, but she wasn't sleeping. She could hear the conversation between them. She pulled her hand slowly away from Helen, and opened her eyes with the intention of visiting only briefly.

"Hello, Helen," she said in a sleepy voice.

Before Helen could answer, Nurse Appleton said, "Mary is scheduled for several tests in fifteen minutes, so please keep your visit short." With that, she left the room.

Mary had been gathering strength a little every day, even though her focus wasn't as clear as it used to be, her hearing and thinking functioned well. She wasn't having any problem hearing what Helen had to say. And, she wanted to know what her former mother-in-law had to say.

Helen again took her hand in hers and said, "Mary, I just had to see you. Carl and I were terribly upset when we learned about your accident. Is there anything we can do?"

Mary remained cautious. Helen had a way of sounding genuine. She tried to shake her head no, but pain prevented it. *There's nothing you can do. Not you, Helen, never you!*

Nurse Albertson had straightened and fluffed up Mary's pillows which allowed her to sit up and lean comfortably against the hospital bed. In doing so, Mary had a close view of Helen's eyes and facial expressions. As hard as she tried to find kindness and tenderness in the face before her, it was impossible. Helen's intentions showed in each word she uttered and it was only a matter of time before she reached her purpose for being there.

"Mary dear, could we be friends again? Peter would want us to. He always loved you, Mary. He even thought about you when making out his will."

Mary shuddered. The last thing she wanted to think about was Peter's will and she didn't care about what Peter wanted. *Here I lay, maybe a hopeless cripple for the rest of my life, and all she wants to talk about is Peter's will? Please get out of here, Helen.*

Helen Randall never got the opportunity to bring up the desired brooch. As she finished her sentence, Grace walked in. Taken aback upon seeing Helen, Grace's hand went to her heart and she said the first thing that came into her mind, "What are you doing here, Helen?"

"My, what a cordial greeting, Grace"

At that moment, Nurse Albertson came into the room with a gurney and two assistants. "Excuse me, ladies, but it's time for Mary's tests. Nurse Albertson turned to Grace as she pushed the gurney into the hall and said, "Mrs. Bryant, Mary should be back in about an hour."

"It will be a good time for me to grab a little lunch, thank you," answered Grace.

Helen turned and followed Grace out of the room. Grabbing Grace's arm, Helen smiled sweetly and said, "Let's have lunch together. We can talk."

As much as I would love to refuse, it might be a good idea to find out what she's up to, especially since she's made a special trip to the hospital to see Mary. Her own daughter waited days after her surgery before she showed up.

Silently, they stood before the elevator doors. When they opened, Grace pushed the button for the cafeteria on the first floor. When they exited the elevator, the aroma of hot food filled the long hall stimulating their appetite. Grace and Helen entered without speaking a word until they stood reading the menu over the food counter.

Helen made the first move. "Do you think a chicken salad sandwich sounds good? Or would you rather have something hot?"

Grace answered in an acid voice, "Order what you want, Helen. I'm still deciding."

Helen selected a tray and silverware wrapped in a napkin. Not long after, Grace followed doing the same thing. Each holding a salad and iced tea made their way to a small table. Helen insisted on paying the cashier. While Grace poured her dressing over the salad, she asked "Helen, did you get a chance to talk to Mary?"

"Actually no, there were too many interruptions."

"What did you want? Maybe, I can help you," suggested Grace in a haphazard way, hoping to take the burden from Mary by getting rid of Helen.

"Did I have to want something to visit Mary?" Helen answered while holding a napkin over her pearls. "After all, Grace, she was my daughter-in-law at one time, and in fact, I feel she still is."

Grace laid her fork down on the dish. Without hesitation, she said, "Helen, let's be realistic. Mary stopped being your daughter-in-law six years ago. You never made any effort to get in touch with her after the divorce because it was not your desire to continue a friendship that didn't include Peter. Now that Peter is dead, we would rather leave things as they are. Besides, our full concentration right now is on getting Mary well and home. Perhaps, you should tell me your real reason for coming here this morning?"

Grace had no intention of wasting words. Helen avoided eye contact, as she handled her pearls and looked down at her half-eaten chicken salad sandwich.

"Peter's lawyer called me. Peter left Mary

the Rolex watch in his will. She had given it to him before they were married. He wanted her to have it. I was merely trying to convey that message to Mary. When I heard about the accident, I honestly wanted to visit her and tell her about the watch."

Grace's intuition assured her Helen didn't tell it all. She finished her salad and rose. "I want to visit with Mary now, Helen. Maybe, we'll run into each other sometime in the future." Grace picked up her purse and walked out.

As Helen watched Grace leave, she stared into the open-door hall for a moment and then walked over to the counter and bought a pack of cigarettes. She had been trying for weeks to break her smoking habit. *I'm never going to be able to give this habit up with all this aggravation*, she mused. She wasn't licked, though, as she smiled about her victory in letting Grace think there was only one item willed to Mary. The brooch was never mentioned.

* * *

Mary was back in her room when Grace walked in. She stopped and stared at her daughter. The bandages had been removed from Mary's head. A fuzz of auburn hair lay neatly on her scalp and the color was beautiful. But, she didn't miss the incision still visible on the right side of her head where doctors took samples of small portions of tissue. With tears in her eyes, Grace extended her arms, and gathered Mary close to her.

"You're going to be fine, dear. God loves you."

Mary returned Grace's smile. "But my legs, Mom, they won't be easy.

The results of the tests will probably be forwarded to Dr. Gordon in a couple of days. Pray something can be done that will keep me from being a cripple the rest of my life."

"Keep the faith, Mary. Everything is going to be fine, you will see."

Grace straightened the bed pillows and Mary closed her eyes. After a few seconds, Mary said "What did Helen want?"

Grace waited a few minutes to collect her thoughts before answering.

"She's up to something, Mary. I think she's scheming for a reason."

Mary squinted and turned her head slowly to hear Grace better.

"What do you mean she's scheming?"

"She said Peter left his Rolex watch to you in his will. Now, tell me would she come all the way over to tell you that. Peter's lawyer could have handled it. There has to be more or she wouldn't have come over here to soften you up."

"I'm not real clear on this, Mom, but I remember something - a phone call, or a meeting I was supposed to have with Peter's lawyer, but I can't remember his name. He was supposed to tell me about two items that were in the will. Didn't Helen mention another item?"

"No, and there my dear, is the crux of the matter. It must be something she wants to get her hands on and doesn't want you to have."

"Yes, and in not mentioning it, we would never know the difference, thinking Peter just willed the watch, like I want the watch. It's engraved to Peter and I want to forget him, not have anything that reminds me of him."

"You just get well, Mary, and I will take care of this. I think it's possible to find out that Peter's lawyer is and then call him. Okay?"

"Good thinking, Mom – Okay."

Mary's eyes closed into a deep sleep as Grace turned to lift her purse from the side table. She tiptoed out of the room.

Eight

*R*eed slipped into his BMW, checked his watch and turned the key in the ignition.

It was seven o'clock in the morning and he wanted an early start at the office. The car phone rang. Lifting the receiver from the hanging hook, he heard "Good morning, dear. How is Mary today?" It was Phoebe.

"Hi Mom."

Reed sensed his mother's surprise since he very seldom called her "Mom," but he knew she liked it.

"Tell me about Mary, Son. How's she doing?"

"She's made wonderful progress. Why don't you go up to the hospital to see her? Hey, Mom, what do you know about Helen Randall?"

"Not too much. As Helen Clark, she was very ambitious. Rumors were that she liked high society and social status. The kids had to be in private schools. Many said she married Carl Randall for money, but who's to say that wasn't just gossip. Why do you ask, Reed?"

"She's in and out of Mary's life and it's

not good. Grace called me last night to say Helen showed up at the hospital. She said she'd give me more detail later. The only other thing she said was that Helen hired a lawyer to fight the will. His name is Frank Knight. You know him, don't you?"

"Yes, of course. He can be trouble, Reed. Your Dad had a few rounds with him."

"I know. Visit Mary, will you, Mom?" Reed said tenderly.

After talking with his mother, Mary was on Reed's mind, so he dialed Grace. Grace answered immediately. She was always an early riser so a phone call at seven or seven-thirty in the morning was not unusual for her.

A slight quiver came through as she said, "Hello."

"Grace, this is Reed. Are you going to the hospital this morning?"

"I'm not going, Reed, until this afternoon, probably around one o'clock. I have some investigating to do this morning," Grace displayed a light lilt to her voice.

"Wow, who or what are you investigating?" which was exactly what Grace wanted him to ask.

"Can you talk a few minutes, Reed?"

"I'm on my car phone driving to work, so talk away, Grace."

"As I mentioned earlier, Helen Randall visited Mary at the hospital yesterday."

Annoyance showed in Grace's voice. "She tried to convince me while we ate lunch in the cafeteria that she came to see Mary because she was concerned about her. Now, Reed that is a lot of humbug! She never bothered with Mary after they divorced, but now she claims Peter's lawyer wants to make sure the Rolex watch is returned to Mary. Humbug, I say again. Mary doesn't give a hoot about that Rolex watch and Helen would not pursue the issue over a watch. There has to be more to it."

Reed listened attentively with one hand on the wheel and the other holding the phone. When she got to the part about Peter's lawyer, Reed felt he knew who she was talking about.

When Grace ended her story, Reed said, "I'm pretty sure that's Frank Knight, but we can find out definitely by calling Patty. She would have the name and time marked on Mary's calendar if she had an appointment set up with him. I'll check it out when I get to the office, unless you want to call Patty."

"Yes, Reed, I'll call. She may have some other information that Mary needs to know, but thank you for offering."

"Tell you what, I'll pick you up about twelve forty-five and we'll shoot over to see Mary. Okay?"

"I'll be ready, but be sure you tell the young man who has been coming to get me each day not to show up."

Reed made a left into the parking lot of the newspaper building. "Okay! Bye."

* * *

When Reed left his office for the afternoon, he slowly pulled out of his parking space with thoughts about Peter Clark. He remembered Peter as fun loving, with a full head of straight blonde hair combed to the side. He mostly remembered his smile; a large mouth that opened to even, bright white teeth. He always had a beautiful woman with him before he married Mary. Reed had met Peter in an economics class in his last year of college.

He recollected how Peter flaunted his wealth. He loved to gamble and was always involved in high betting at the numerous social events. It didn't matter whether it was a simple game of pool or a game of golf. He remembered his bragging about going to Las Vegas every May to pick up some extra cash.

Reed took him with a grain of salt and on occasion, Peter would call him for a night out. He could still hear a remark Peter made once on a golf course when Reed mentioned studying for an exam. "Not me, Man," he said. "I didn't even want to be in that class, but my mother insisted on it." He was smart, however, and sailed through to graduation with flying colors.

After leaving college, Reed settled down to help his dad at the newspaper and lost contact with Peter. He was honestly surprised when he received an invitation to his wedding. He was also amazed that there was a woman who could settle him down long enough to get married.

Nine

*A*fter talking to Reed, Grace decided to call Patty. It was quarter to eight, but Patty, like Mary, was an early worker. She dialed Mary's office and longed for the day when Mary would be back, well and healthy again.

"Mary Bryant-Clark's office!"

"Patty, this is Grace Bryant. How are you?"

"Mrs. Bryant. How nice to hear your voice again. How is Mary?"

"She is out of her comatose state, Patty. This is truly a blessing, but we won't know what is decided on her legs for a few days yet. Pray that they can fix them again in surgery. Visitors are allowed now, so if you're interested, she would love to see you."

"I'd love to see her, too. I'll work out something to get over to the hospital."

"Patty, would you know the name of the lawyer who called Mary just before her accident? She remembers setting up a time to meet with him, but can't remember his name. Would you have a record of that appointment?"

"Let's see, Mrs. Bryant. Yes, his secretary called me because Mary didn't show up for the appointment. Somehow, I overlooked calling him to tell about her accident.

After that, I wrote it here on the calendar. It was ten- thirty on the 23rd with Frank Knight. Do you want his telephone number?"

"Yes, please Patty."

After writing Frank Knight's telephone number down, Grace asked if there were any messages for Mary. Patty promised she'd bring any information or new developments to Mary when she went to see her.

* * *

Grace waited until nine o'clock and then punched in Frank Knight's number.

"Good Morning. Frank Knight's Office."

"Could I speak to Mr. Knight?" asked Grace. She hoped the nervousness didn't show in her voice.

"Who's calling, please?"

Grace wanted to think this out carefully before replying so she took a couple of seconds to answer. "This is Grace Bryant, Mary Bryant Clark's mother and she has asked me to call Mr. Knight about an important matter."

"One moment please."

Frank Knight was reading over a case when his intercom buzzed. His secretary relayed the message.

"Put her on,"

"Hello, Mrs. Bryant, this is Frank Knight. How are you today?"

"I am fine, Mr. Knight."

"What can I do for you?" Frank asked as he fumbled through his bottom drawer, searching for Peter Clark's file. He also glanced over to the safe wondering should he tell her about both items. He decided to wait until he heard what was on her mind.

Grace began, "Mary is recovering, but not quite up to handling some situations, so she asked me to call you. It seems she had an appointment with you and because of the accident was unable to keep it. She wants to know the details of the meeting."

"First of all, Mrs. Bryant," "How is Mary? Is she still in the hospital?"

It seemed to Grace that he was sincere, so she took the time to report on Mary's prognosis. She ended with ". . . so before having her leg surgery, she is trying to catch up on loose ends; therefore, the purpose of the call."

"I see. Well, Mrs. Bryant, the meeting would have pertained to Peter Clark's will. He had given Mary a brooch." Grace took a deep breath while Frank decided to tell all and let the chips fall where they may. "It was given to him by his grandmother. Mary returned it when they divorced. Also, there is a Rolex watch involved that was given to Peter from Mary and he requested it be returned to her."

"Funny, Mr. Knight," Grace said sarcastically, "Helen Randall never mentioned the brooch."

"When was that, Mrs. Bryant?"

"Yesterday, she came to see Mary at the hospital and we had lunch together.

She talked about the watch, but didn't say a word about the brooch." Grace ended her remark with, "Somehow, I don't think that was an oversight on her part."

"Hmmm . . . it's a very expensive item, Mrs. Bryant, and she wants to keep it in the family. She's not happy that Peter gave it to Mary without her permission."

Grace decided to go one step further, "Mary returned it to Peter after the divorce, and for Peter to will it to Mary means he really wanted her to have it. Don't you think?"

"Yes, I would say so."

"I am seeing Mary this afternoon, Mr. Knight, so I will bring her up to date on this matter. I would like to know her feelings on the brooch. Can I get back to you on this?"

"Certainly! By the way, Mrs. Bryant, if Mary is up to it you may want her to assign you the power of attorney so you can handle her affairs until she is well."

Grace made no comment on this suggestion and closed the conversation with

"Thanks for giving me your time." She couldn't wait to see Mary. There was a lot to tell her.

Reed was on time, and Grace slipped into the passenger seat of the BMW.

Her lime green two-piece suit, set off with a bright floral scarf twirled around her neck, flattered her graying short bobbed hair style. Reed made a point to comment on how nice she looked.

"Thank you." She then proceeded to tell Reed all about her conversation with Frank Knight.

"So, it's a brooch, is it?" Reed said like he was exposing a deep, dark secret.

"It must be worth a fortune if she wants it back so badly."

"Frank Knight said it was very expensive and Helen wants to keep it in the family, but Peter has given it to Mary twice, so rightfully, it belongs to her. And, it was never given to Helen. Peter's grandmother gave it to him originally."

"I see, and are you going to tell Mary all about this today?"

"I certainly am. Her mind seems to be working well now, but I hope she can grasp the seriousness of this situation. I want to know her feelings. I'm not sure whether she will say, let's fight it or let her have it. We will see."

Ten

*L*arge sprays of impatiens were beautifully arranged around the front entrance of Rockford Memorial Hospital as Reed and Grace pulled up. "Go on in, Grace, and I'll be with you shortly."

Grace's step was lively as she got out of the car knowing Mary felt better. Reed drove off to find a parking place.

The smell of fresh lilacs, sitting in a vase on the Information Desk, caught Grace's attention as she entered the foyer of the hospital. She smiled taking in their aroma, and pushed the up button at the elevator doors. She exited on the third floor and headed for Room 312. Mary was alone and sleeping.

Nurse Albertson saw Grace enter and walked into the room, whispering softly to Grace. "She's had a battery of tests on her legs this morning and is probably tired."

"I'll be back," Grace said. "She can sleep for a while."

Grace met Reed in the lobby of the hospital and together they went to the small cafeteria on the first floor for a cup of coffee. There they found Phoebe, who also was waiting for Mary to recover.

"Well, for goodness sakes! Look who's here?" said Reed smiling. He was delighted to see his mother. Grace and Phoebe exchanged greetings.

"Do you think we can all visit her at the same time? If not, I can come back tomorrow," said Phoebe. "She may not want too much company."

Grace answered, "Let's see first. She may feel fine after sleeping. I'm sure she'd like to see you." After about a half hour chat, they took the elevator up to Mary's room.

* * *

In a different part of town at the same time Reed, Grace, and Phoebe entered Mary's room, Frank Knight's intercom buzzed.

"It's Helen Randall, Mr. Knight, on line two."

Frank wanted badly to say tell her I'm not here, but instead said, "Ok, put her through."

"Hello, Helen. How are you today?"

Helen let Frank's question go and got to the point immediately, "Have you had any contact with Mary Bryant?"

"Mary needs more time before handling particular affairs, according to her mother. But I have had a discussion with Grace

Bryant about the items willed to her."

"That girl will never be able to handle "particular affairs," again, Frank. She would never know the difference whether you gave her the brooch or not, so just take it out of the will," Helen was adamant. "What did you discuss with Grace?"

"Grace is handling Mary's affairs until she is capable of handling them herself. She has improved considerably, by Grace's report, but will need leg surgery. I have told Grace that there are two items in the will for Mary and she knows about the brooch. This is a legal matter, Helen, and I cannot just take the brooch out of the will. If Mary decides to give it back to you that will be her decision and not mine. Grace will give Mary a full report of our conversation. If you want to deal with them, that's your business, but leave me out of it."

Frank was emphatic and felt he had made himself clear. Not being a very patient person, Helen slammed the phone down. Walking back to her garden, she began to contrive another devious plan.

* * *

Upon entering Mary's room, Reed, Grace and Phoebe were delighted to see her sitting up, wearing makeup, and smiling. Some of Mary's thick, ruddy hair had returned. The areas shaved for surgery were barely noticeable. She was beginning to look like her old self again. Her eyes sparkled and seemed bluer than ever to Reed.

Grace leaned over and gave her a big hug and Reed followed with a kiss on the cheek, smelling a perfumed soap or powder that made him want more. Mary sparkled when she saw Phoebe and made a special point to remark how lovely she looked. They held hands and a constant conversation carried on between them for several minutes. Phoebe had brought a bouquet of flowers and a nurse followed up with a vase. She visited with Mary for a short while and then decided to let Reed and Grace have a turn. Before she left, she kissed Mary on the forehead and patted her hand.

Grace gave a full report to Mary regarding her phone call to Frank Knight. Reed listened, saying nothing. Finally Mary said, "Maybe I should just let her have the brooch. It means a lot more to her than it does to me. If only she wasn't so greedy. She really doesn't deserve a generous decision."

"Wait a minute," said Reed. Why do you think Peter wanted you to have it?

When you returned it the first time, he could have easily given it to his mother, but he insisted on you having it by placing it in his will. There must have been a reason for that."

Grace added to the conversation by saying, "Maybe he knew something about Helen that we don't know."

"Do you remember anything at all, Mary, about the relationship between Helen Randall and Peter's grandmother?" asked Reed.

Mary pondered a minute and said, "Only that they didn't get along very well. I remember arguments between them when we were married. Nothing specific though."

"It's also strange that the grandmother would give the brooch to Peter and not his sister, Karen," concluded Reed.

"What do you mean?" asked Grace.

"Well," said Reed. "Karen could wear the brooch, whereas, Peter would eventually give it to his wife. He certainly wouldn't wear it."

Mary chimed in with, "Peter was her favorite. He would hug her and swing her around and she loved that. The others hardly bothered with her."

As the conversation continued, Dr. Gordon came into the room. Grace asked if they should leave so he could examine Mary.

"No, no," he said. "I want you all to know that we will do the first surgery on Mary's legs Tuesday morning, around eight o'clock."

Turning to Mary, he continued. "We have gone over your x-rays, and the possibilities are good for straightening that right leg, but your therapy will be long, and you will have to be very patient. Dr. Russell Cherny is the orthopedic doctor who will perform the surgery and he comes highly recommended. So, you will be in good hands and I will be around to see that everything goes well. He will be in to see you tomorrow to give you more details. Any questions?"

"Can I see Mary before she goes into surgery, doctor?" asked Grace.

"Of course, be here by seven o'clock. The surgery will probably take a good four or five hours. Are you ready for this, Mary?" Dr. Gordon asked.

Mary looked down at her legs and then up at Dr. Gordon and nodded yes.

Reed took her hand and after Dr. Gordon left, he said, "I think it's time for you to rest now, Mary. We will be back again tomorrow." This time Reed bent down, lifted her chin and kissed her on the lips, taking in again the sweet scent of her fragrance.

After dropping Grace off, Reed went back to the office. It was three o'clock.

He checked with Susie to see if there were any messages. Taking his usual collection of messages into his office, he began to flip through them as his phone rang. It was Cheryl.

"Hello, stranger," she said. "What's taking up all your time lately or maybe I should say, who?" Reed lifted his eyes up and shook his head.

"I've been busy," he answered.

"You know, Reed, this is June - early June, and we do have a wedding coming up in September. There are more things to be done. I can't do them all by myself. I need your help, darling!"

"Cheryl, we need to talk. Can we have dinner one night this week?"

There was dead silence on the other end of the phone and finally Cheryl said, "Reed, why?"

Reed felt a stab in the pit of his stomach, but he knew it would not be easy with Cheryl. She would fight back.

Reed's old habit took over and he ran his fingers through his hair, cleared his throat and said softly, "I can't marry you, Cheryl." It was the first time he had said anything softly to Cheryl in a long time.

The phone seemed to go dead. Reed finally had to say, "Are you there, Cheryl?"

Only one answer came out of Cheryl after the long silence, "You son of a bitch!"

She hung up immediately.

* * *

After Cheryl hung up, tears swelled and overflowed. She picked up the glass vase on the patio table filled with long stem red roses and crashed it on the beautiful inlaid bricks that ran the length of the terrace. Then she ran; she ran the full length of the long lush garden and threw herself down under a huge oak tree and sobbed, pounding her fists on the ground.

Reed, in the meantime, heard the phone click on the other end and dropped his head. He had never felt so low and disgusted with himself before. He realized how much planning had gone into the wedding, but to marry Cheryl would be a huge mistake. He really didn't want to tell her such awful news by phone, but he also knew he didn't love her. He finally admitted to himself that he loved Mary. There was nothing he could do for Cheryl now, except to just leave it alone.

But, Cheryl was not about to leave it alone. She pulled herself up off the ground and walked straight and tall into the house. After dressing in a floral outfit with a pink short jack and matching pink shoes, Cheryl jumped into her black Volvo 840 and drove to Rockford Memorial Hospital. Checking the desk for Mary's room number, Cheryl pushed the elevator button. As she peeked into Mary's room, she found her sitting up watching television. It was six o'clock and the first time Cheryl had checked the time. Probably her dinner time, thought Cheryl, but she walked in anyway.

"Hi, Mary, hope I'm not startling you."

"Oh, Cheryl, this is a surprise. But please come in and sit down."

Cheryl Cunningham was the last person Mary would expect to visit her. "Is this your dinner time?"

Mary looked at the clock on the table next to her bed and answered, "Soon, but don't leave because of that."

Cheryl had to admit that even with the accident and all Mary had been through, she was beautiful. *But that's no reason for her to steal my man,* she thought.

"Reed told me about your accident and I happened to be in the area…thought I'd stop in to see you. Hope you don't mind." Cheryl's smile followed her remark.

"Not at all!" Mary was beginning to realize this was not a casual visit between friends. Something was brewing and she hoped it would come out in conversation.

"I would like to tell you, Mary, that I'm sorry you're not my wedding correspondent any longer. Don't get me wrong, Carol Langley's doing a good job, but it's too bad I have to dismiss her."

Mary, starting to reach for a box of tissues resting on her side table, stopped in mid-air and turned to look at Cheryl. "I beg your pardon. Did you say you have to dismiss her?"

"Yes," Cheryl said slowly. "You see, Mary, there isn't going to be a wedding.

I've been dumped by Reed. Can you imagine, after all these years, he doesn't love me anymore. My goodness, I find it hard to believe that after going through school together and spending practically all of our growing up years together, he doesn't love me anymore? Do you want to know why, Mary?"

Mary didn't answer, just sat dumbfounded.

"Because, a red-head beauty has worked her charm on him and he thinks he loves her. Don't do this to me, Mary. Reed is mine. You could never give him what I can. He's not a pizza and beer guy. He's accustomed to champagne."

Cheryl had not bothered to sit down; turning on her heels she wiggled her fingers goodbye and walked out.

Mary was devastated. The hospital aide had brought dinner in and placed it on her portable table. She sat and stared at it. Her appetite was gone. She reached for the phone and called Grace.

"Mom," she choked out. Then, cleared her throat and said, "Can you give me Reed's home telephone number?"

"Of course, dear, is something wrong?"

"No, I just want to talk to him."

Mary didn't want to talk about it or explain at this time. She would tell Grace another time.

After hanging up with Grace, Mary punched in Reed's home number. It was after six, nearly six thirty, and she felt he might be there. Reed answered.

"Reed, here," was his reply as he munched on a piece of sourdough bread.

"Reed, this is Mary. I need to talk to you. It's important!"

"You sound serious, Mary, is something wrong?"

"Yes, Reed, there is something wrong."

A slight tremble in her voice might have given her away as she said, "Can you come during the eight o'clock visiting hour this evening? What is to be discussed I would rather not discuss on the phone or in front of my mother."

"Sure, Mary, I'll be there."

Reed worried immediately. Could she have gotten some bad news on her legs?

He didn't know what to think. He ate a quick dinner and jumped into the shower.

Thirty minutes later, he pulled into the parking lot of the hospital and found his favorite spot. *So many more available in the evening,* he thought. He had stopped at a florist and bought Mary six beautiful red roses; grabbing them off the seat of the car, he began to find his way to the hospital entrance.

He found Mary reading People Magazine as he crept into the room quietly. She lowered the magazine and he could see tears welling in the corner of her eyes.

"Mary, what in the world is wrong?" He was terribly disturbed. "Have you had some bad news on the surgery?"

Mary collected herself and said, "No. I had a visit from Cheryl Cunningham earlier this evening."

Reed couldn't believe what he was hearing. "What the hell did she want?"

Mary hesitated a few seconds trying desperately to control her shaky hands. "What she wanted, Reed, was to tell me you didn't love her anymore be ... cause, you were taken in by a red-headed vixen that used her magic to lure you.

In other words, I deliberately stole you away from her, a stealing I know nothing about.

She told me it wasn't going to work, because you like champagne rather than beer, or some nonsense like that. What is this all about, Reed? I may have had a severe brain injury, but damn it, I'm not brain dead."

The tears overflowed and dribbled down Mary's face.

Reed couldn't find words. After a long

silence, he felt an emotion he couldn't explain. His stomach contracted and a lump swelled up in his throat. He couldn't speak. He fell back on his old habit of flipping his straight brown hair back. He had no idea what or how to say anything. "I told her I couldn't marry her. That's all."

"After all the wedding arrangements and plans that have been made, what made you say that?"

"Because - - -". Mary's wet, blue eyes just stared at him. "Because I've fallen in love with you- - - and Grace."

Mary closed her eyes and the tears dribbled down again, and Reed took her hand and kissed it. Sitting down in a comfortable old chair next to her bed, Reed said, "Could you love me, Mary? I'm not always kind and sometimes even crabby, but I will love you until my dying day with white hair or bald."

Mary had to laugh in spite of the tears. She reached down and took his face into her two hands, "I have loved you since I first saw you. You may not have a vixen on your hands, but you could possibly have a cripple. Are you sure you want that?"

"I want what you want. Together, Mary, we'll lick this, and you won't only walk again, you'll run."

Mary bent down and kissed Reed. As he lifted himself up to gather her in his arms,

Mary's left leg moved for the first time since the accident. She pulled away and shouted, "REED, REED, MY LEG, THIS ONE, IS MOVING." The excitement was overwhelming for both of them.

Before Reed left, he said, "Mary, I will take care of Cheryl Cunningham. Don't worry; you'll not hear from her again.

Mary smiled and answered, "Tell her you prefer beer."

* * *

Grace arrived at exactly seven o'clock Tuesday morning to see Mary before her surgery. Mary was waiting for her. She told Grace as soon as she entered the room about the movement of her leg, but she held off telling Grace anything about loving Reed. She wanted to savor the remembrance of it for a little while. But this morning, she would bring Grace in on the happiness of it all. When Grace walked into her room, a tender smile crossed Mary's face. Grace was delighted to see her in such a good mood.

"Well, you sure are happy about going into surgery," Grace said cheerfully. "I expected to see you worried and scared."

"No, Mom, I decided to take a positive approach that everything is going to be just fine. Having my left leg come alive has changed my whole outlook on my recovery.

Also, falling in love hasn't been bad either."
Mary chuckled as Grace frowned.

"What are you talking about, falling in love?"

"Just that, Mom, I have fallen in love with someone very special and what's more he loves me, too. Can you guess who?"

Removing her chic turned-up straw hat with an artificial daisy sewn in the back, Grace sat on the edge of Mary's bed. She looked stunning once again in a bright blue two piece dress. She thought briefly and then said, "I think I know who."

Mary could never imagine how pleased Grace was for she loved Reed as well.

To have him as a son-in-law would be the ultimate prize. Just as these thoughts came into her head, so did the gurney being pushed by Nurse Albertson.

"Time to go, Mary," Nurse Albertson said before turning her attention to Grace. "Dr. Cherny will see you in the waiting room after the surgery, Mrs. Bryant. He has given Mary a brief explanation of the surgery, but she asked him to save the details until after the surgery, so that she, Reed and you could all listen at the same time."

Dr. Cherny followed the gurney into the room and said, "We'll do better than that, Mary, we are going to film your surgery so you, too, can watch the procedure used. You'll find it fascinating."

Eleven

*F*rank Knight called his wife to tell her he would be working late. He bought a "take-out" dinner from Kentucky Fried Chicken and returned to his office to finish some backlogged work. Around nine o'clock, he decided enough was enough, turned the light out on his desk, locked up and left.

A half hour after he left, a key pushed into the lock of his office door, turned and twisted, then opened the huge door containing Frank's name. Dressed in black from head to toe, the intruder headed right for the bookcase.

With gloved fingers, the books were removed from the bookcase that concealed the safe. The safe opened as the code numbers were dialed and the manila envelope containing the brooch and watch were lifted. Carefully locking the safe and putting the books back on the bookcase a quick hand stuffed the envelope into a black bag and left, making sure to lock the door on the way out. So perfectly planned, the whole crime scene took no more than fifteen seconds.

The next morning, Frank ran from his car in the pouring rain, arriving in his office around nine o'clock. He removed his wet raincoat, opened the dripping umbrella to dry, and ran his fingers through his wet hair. He sat down at his desk to begin his usual morning routine. His intercom buzzed and his secretary announced that Helen Randall was on the phone.

"Put her on,"

"Frank," Helen dragged out. "Is this too early for you?"

"Not at all, Helen, I am accustomed to early hours. What's on your mind?" he asked, with compunction.

"Would you have time this afternoon to meet with me and my lawyer? He'd like to see the items left in the will to Mary. He's especially interested in the brooch. We could come to your office around two o'clock. Is that all right with you?"

"Let's see," Frank eyed his calendar. "Yes, that will be fine. See you then."

He thought about checking the safe when the phone rang again. It was a client call he expected. When he hung up, he forgot about the safe since it wasn't his top priority for the day. After lunch, he got involved in a current case pending before the courts and almost forgot about Helen and her lawyer, until his secretary buzzed him to say they were there. He rose from his chair, opened the office door and extended his hand to welcome them.

Helen introduced her lawyer as Clifford Lakes and Frank asked them to sit down.

Frank returned to his oak desk and started to sit, but suddenly remembered the safe and its valuable items. Straightening, he walked over to the bookcase, removed the books and opened the safe. Knowing exactly where he had placed them, he extended his hand into the safe but the envelope wasn't there. He ran his hand all over the safe, pulled out a couple of other items, even retrieved a small flashlight from his desk and flashed it into the safe, but nothing was there!

He began to perspire and distrust himself. *Could he have put them somewhere else?*

Helen said, "What's wrong, Frank?"

"I'm not quite sure. I need to check my desk," he answered, convinced that he had put the two items in the safe. After ransacking his desk and finding nothing, he sat back in his brown leather chair, perspiring profusely.

"What is the problem, Frank?" asked Helen sternly.

Out of breath and completely rattled, Frank uttered, "I can't find them."

Helen glanced at her lawyer for a moment. "Don't tell me you are looking frantically for the brooch and watch?"

Frank answered very softly, "Yes. I know

they were in my safe. I am the only one who knows the code to that safe and I did not take them out."

"Well, Frank, they didn't break out. If no one else knows the code, how could they be gone?"

Clifford Lakes sat silently in a matching brown leather chair facing Frank's desk.

Speaking softly, he said, "Could they be in your briefcase?"

"If they are," said Frank. "I have no idea how they got there."

He immediately started going through his briefcase but with no success. He sat on the edge of his chair and slumped. "I'm just devastated. I can't imagine how this happened. Someone had to have tampered with that safe. I'm calling the police."

Frank lifted the receiver and dialed 911.

Helen and Clifford Lakes sat stunned. The impact of this predicament began to sink in, and Helen flushed with anger. Gritting her teeth, she leaned into Frank's face. "Frank Knight, you better find that brooch or I will put you out of business, if not run you out of Rockford. You'll never handle another case."

Frank knew she could do it, too. He had no recourse, no retort. He stared at Helen while the perspiration ran down his back.

Grabbing her Gucci bag and flinging it over her shoulder, Helen turned to Clifford

Lakes and said harshly, "Let's go, Clifford."

* * *

The surgery on Mary's right leg took over five hours. Reed and Grace had sent her into the operating room with kisses and support. They spent their time either in the hospital coffee shop or walking the garden grounds. At noon, they had lunch, and at one o'clock returned to the waiting room with anticipation for news about Mary soon. At one-fifteen, Grace looked up from her magazine to see Dr. Cherny in full operating garb looking around for them. She poked Reed and together they rose to meet him.

"Mary is doing fine," reported Dr. Cherny. She's in Intensive Care right now and I suggest you wait about an hour before going in to see her. She's still completely out and should start coming around by then. In order to straighten the leg, we had to put a steel rod in her ankle and run a support down the length of her leg which screws into the rod. We filmed the whole procedure, which you can watch at your convenience. Her recovery will take months with constant therapy. That's about all I can tell you now. Much of what happens next will depend on Mary and how well she heals." He shook hands with Reed, smiled to Grace and was gone.

Reed and Grace looked at each other, said nothing, and sat down to wait another hour. After a short time, Grace turned to Reed who looked up from his newspaper.

"How about coming home with me for a nice dinner after we leave here? Does a glass of wine under the willow tree sound good to you?"

Reed smiled at her and eagerly said, "You bet!"

When Reed and Grace entered the ICU Unit they found Mary heavily sedated. They stood at the end of the bed looking down at her. Two nurses buzzed around the bed, one checking her blood pressure and pulse while the other raised her bed, making her breathing easier. While Nurse Albertson lifted the covers on the bed to check the bandaged leg, Grace looked at the IV bottles dripping into Mary's veins and tears settled in the corner of her eyes.

Dr. Cherny's warning about not staying too long came into Reed's mind. Reed took Grace's hand into his and said, "Perhaps we should go."

She nodded and they both left the room, agreeing Mary needed rest more than anything. Maybe she would accept company more readily tomorrow.

They drove to Grace's home in silence. When they entered, Grace immediately went to her room to change and Reed found his way around, stopping in the library where rows of books sat handsomely on mahogany shelves. He bent across a beautiful oak desk and lifted a silver-framed picture of Mary's father and Grace taken in their younger years.

He scanned the bookshelves, and was amazed at the large collection of books the family had accumulated over the years. Reed turned as Grace entered the library.

"Mary's father was certainly a handsome man," he said as he placed the picture back on the desk.

"Indeed, he was. He died of a brain tumor much too young. But, I suppose Mary told you about that."

"No, actually she hadn't. We have a lot of catching up to do."

"Yes you do, but let's put that all aside right now and relax. Would you mind opening a bottle of Chardonnay for me?"

Reed and Grace adjourned to the kitchen. Grace pointed to a drawer where Reed could find a bottle opener. After fumbling around the usual kitchen junk drawer, he found the opener, opened the bottle and poured the wine into two stemmed glasses Grace had put on the counter.

Grace was checking the partially cooked pork roast she had prepared that morning and turned the oven on to finish cooking it. He smiled knowing that she had planned earlier to invite him home for dinner. Even her vegetables were cut, and quartered, soaking in ice water.

After everything appeared under control in the kitchen, she said to Reed, "It's such a beautiful day, let's go sit outdoors." Grace carried her glass of wine while Reed held the door open. He followed with a glass of wine in one hand, the bottle in the other. The snapdragons, impatiens, petunias and pansy arrangements that surrounded the fence in the backyard looked beautiful, and Reed commented on them. But, nothing could replace the breezy comfort of sitting near the willow tree.

"Do you think Mary will be able to come home soon, Reed? It has been such a long time since she's felt the comfort of her home."

"I hope so, Grace," Reed answered. "Let's ask the doctor tomorrow. She has a great deal of therapy to go through and I'm not sure all of that has to be done in the hospital. We need to ask questions. She's been through a lot and we should be grateful for how well she's recovering."

"She told me about you loving one another, and I couldn't be happier. You have been such a comfort to me through this trauma, and I don't know how to thank you," Grace responded while taking small sips of wine.

Reed leaned over and took Grace's hand. "You don't have to thank me. I should thank you for giving me Mary. I know now that I must have loved her more than I realized in order to stay the course of helping you. Later, I knew I loved you both and didn't want to live life without her. I was so close to making a dreadful mistake by marrying the wrong person, and even though I feel like a cad for hurting Cheryl, ruining her life would have been even worse. You see, I couldn't have loved her like I do Mary."

Grace remained silent for a few minutes after hearing such a profession of truth.

Tears built in her eyes, but she brushed them aside and said, "Come, let's have dinner."

Twelve

*W*hen Frank Knight pulled into the driveway of his home, he saw that his wife, Kathryn, was home. Her white Cadillac was in the two-car garage, and as usual, she had left the door up. He drove in on the other side of her car and walked to the driveway to pick up the paper. He pulled the large garage door down. Preferring to enter into the aroma of the kitchen at dinner time, he walked the short distance to the back door. Kathryn, knowing Frank's habits, had left the door open and he found something smelling mighty good cooking on the top range.

Still nervous and rattled from the occurrence of the afternoon, Frank put his briefcase on a chair and walked to the bar in the dining room to make a martini.

Kathryn appeared at that moment and said, "Make one for me too, darling." Reaching up to kiss him, she took his briefcase off the chair and placed it in the foyer by the hall tree.

"Something sure smells good," Frank said. "What's for dinner?"

"One of your favorites, darling. Beef Stroganoff! It can sit for a while. Let's relax over our cocktails."

With that, Frank followed Kathryn into the living room, a fashionable room with a cinnamon-colored couch that stretched the entire length of one wall. The room was decorated in different shades of green with the wall over the couch wallpapered in a collection of huge bright flowers. Kathryn, being an interior decorator in her earlier days, displayed a talent that was professionally envied.

"How was your day, dear?" she asked.

"Not bad. Busy, of course. How was yours?" answered Frank and then the phone rang.

He rose from the navy leather recliner to make another martini and said, "I'll get it."

Kathryn would not allow a phone in the living room because she felt it interrupted intelligent conversation. She insisted it be put in the office off the den. Frank took the call in the office.

"Hello." There was a silence and then he said, "I told you never to call me here. I know, I know. I went through the whole embarrassment this afternoon and convinced them. I can't talk to you now. Where can I call you tomorrow?"

Frank wrote a number on a pad next to the phone, then said goodbye.

"Dinner's ready, Frank, any bad news there?"

"No, Kathryn, just a client calling too late."

* * *

The next morning Reed called Grace. "Hello Grace," he greeted when she answered the phone. "I have work at the office that has to be finished this morning. I could pick you up at one o'clock to take you to the hospital if you would like."

Grace hesitated, "No. I think I should spend the entire day with Mary in case she needs someone nearby to help her when the nurses aren't in the room."

"I well understand," Reed said. "I'll send your regular driver to your house whenever you choose and I will join you later in the day."

"That is very kind of you to offer. I would like to be at the hospital by nine-thirty if that is convenient."

After ending their conversation, Grace donned a colorful outfit with the hope of lifting Mary's spirits.

When Grace arrived at the hospital she found her daughter still sedated and drowsy. Nurse Albertson told her Mary had a great deal of pain throughout the night and sedation was necessary.

Grace pulled a chair to the side of the bed

and stroked Mary's arm. From time to time, she would wet a washcloth with cool water and wipe her face. Mary was covered with a light sheet and Grace could see the thick bandages that wrapped her leg from the hip down and covered the entire foot. Fear gripped her heart as she sat worrying. She stayed at Mary's bedside, listening to her moaning and watching her painful facial expressions. More than once, Grace wiped the tears streaming down her cheeks.

Two plastic bags of fluid hooked up on the right side of the bed dripped into Mary's veins. Grace wondered if she would ever be herself again. She bent her head down on the bed and prayed.

* * *

Helen Randall was furious as she said goodbye to Clifford Lakes. He dropped her off at home and drove off. She stormed into the foyer and let the front door slam. Her face was flushed with anger and her hat was askew.

She didn't want Carl Randall to know anything about the brooch, the watch, Peter's will or Frank Knight. Her goal was to get the brooch back and she did not want any advice from Carl or anyone else, but when he heard the door slam, he came in from the screened porch to see what was going on. His white hair and handsome face were complimented with horn-rimmed glasses which he removed and held in one hand.

"Are you all right, Helen? What seems to be the problem?"

"Nothing," Helen snapped back.

"Something is wrong." His gentle nature expressed a concern and he approached her kindly, "Maybe I can help. You wouldn't be angry over nothing."

Helen, wishing desperately to dismiss the whole thing, asked, "What makes you think something's wrong?"

"Well, for one thing your hat is on crooked."

With that, Helen yanked it off of her head and flipped it onto the center table in the foyer, not cracking a smile. She saw Carl grin as he put the newspaper under his arm.

He reached for her hand and led her into the softly decorated, comfortable parlor that displayed multiple shades of beiges and browns. He sat her down on her favorite recliner and went to the bar. Filling an old-fashioned glass with ice, Carl poured some Jameson whiskey over the cubes and handed it to her.

Helen was determined not to tell Carl about the afternoon fiasco. "I was just annoyed, Carl, with Karen. I had spoken to her on the car phone and she always seems to have an excuse for not attending our holiday get-togethers. I was thinking about a July 4th party on our grounds, and of course, she has other plans."

"Don't let that upset you, Helen. She may change her mind."

* * *

Frank Knight decided to make a call. "Yeah, it's me, Frank," he said into the mouth piece. "Can you talk? So, everything went okay - no hang ups in opening the safe? Good for you! I have to convince the police that the burglary was done by a professional, since there was no break-in. Just lay low and stay out of the picture as much as possible. I will handle the rest. Oh, and don't call me at home. I will call you if something comes up. Put those two items in a very safe place, okay? Yeah, bye."

Frank hung up and drove straight to his office with success written all over his face. His thoughts were menacing. *Someone is going to pay dearly to own that brooch.*

Thirteen

*W*hile Grace was at Mary's bedside, Reed was attending an annual Voice of Business Luncheon held at the Ramada Suites. He belonged to the First Rockford Group, an organization of businessmen whose companies recently made large investments in the Rockford Area. It was a diversion from his normal newspaper business and he enjoyed it. The luncheon lasted until two o'clock, and he called Susie to see if anything earthshaking was happening before deciding to go to the hospital to see Mary.

Susie reported everything was going along smoothly so he drove straight to the hospital. He entered Mary's room and found Grace. Her eyes were closed as her head rested on the bed and she held Mary's hand. An exhausted look on her face revealed the torture she was going through worrying. He lifted his eyes to look at Mary, and a weakness filled his heart. The pain on her face spoke volumes.

When he put his arm around Grace's shoulders, she opened her eyes and sat up. Reed could see she was too distraught to smile. He watched as she went to the corner sink to wet a washcloth. She returned to the bed and wiped Mary's face with cool water. He said nothing. The enormous amount of bandages under the covers and Mary's groans were more than he could handle. He decided to leave the room.

As he left, Mary's subconscious came alive. *Who's making that awful sound? Someone's in a lot of pain. The light is blinding – Why is the light blinding? I don't need that much light. Thank you for wiping my face. That feels good! There's a desk and a beautiful blonde woman with long hair in a flowered dress throwing roses over a balcony. Who's catching the roses below? Why is the back of his head showing; where's his face? This is so strange, and why is someone still moaning. My God, where am I? So far up and look at that huge tree just floating around. Oh, the pain is back again and thanks, thanks, thanks for wiping my face. Stop moaning! I can't stand that moaning.*

The thrashing went on, and Mary's crying out loud disturbed Grace to a point that she called Nurse Albertson to do something about her pain. Nurse Albertson returned, rolled Mary over and gave her a shot of morphine. Then, the light in Mary's subconscious world went out.

* * *

After Reed left the room, he saw Dr. Cherny coming down the hall and he stopped him.

"Do you have time for a couple of questions, Doctor?" asked Reed.

"Just a couple! I'm on my way to a meeting."

"I just came from Mary's room and she really doesn't look good. Is there any reason to worry?"

"No, the surgery went well. Is her mother here now?"

Reed nodded.

"I'm going to take a few minutes to talk to both of you. Let's go to Mary's room."

Upon entering Mary's room, Dr. Cherny checked Mary's vital signs and lifted the covers to view her leg. This done, he said, "She should open her eyes and come around by tomorrow. I have arranged for her to be a part of The Sports Physical Therapy Program at the Rockford Clinic. It was recently created to provide individualized support for athletes and others who wanted to return to peak condition. Mary might need months of therapy before progress can be realized. She must be willing to endure the long process."

Switching his eyes from Reed to Grace, he said, "Trust me, the surgery went well."

With that, he turned to Reed, shook his hand, smiled at Grace and left.

Reed drove Grace home and again they sat around the willow tree with a glass of wine to calm their nerves. Grace had pulled the round wrought iron table and chairs out from under the tree since the dangling branches started to touch the ground.

"Will you stay for dinner, Reed? I've some cold beef in the refrigerator that would make delicious sandwiches."

"That sounds great, Grace, but I've a lot of paperwork to check and I better go. I'll take you up on that another time."

Reed labored late into the night with thoughts of Mary's condition running through his mind.

* * *

Frank Knight called the police about the burglary. Inspector Bud Adams, a short bald man around fifty, arrived in a badly fitting suit and checked around the office before interrogating Frank. After questioning him on obvious details, he asked if his secretary could come in for some questions. Frank wanted to say no. He didn't want her involved. But in order to avoid suspicion, he allowed it.

Inspector Adams concluded that the secretary knew nothing about the burglary and dismissed her. However, he was baffled about the neatness of the theft. There were no fingerprints, no break-ins, and no disturbance in the office at all. Even the books hiding the safe were put back in their proper place.

"Did you touch this bookshelf or safe since the burglary, Mr. Knight?" asked Inspector Adams.

"No, I have not nor has anyone else, as far as I know."

Adams stood in front of the safe scratching his head, with his suit jacket hanging open. "Whoever did the robbery surely was professional. There isn't a trace of evidence. How do you think the burglar got in?"

Frank hesitated a second and then said, "That's your job to find out. I have no idea."

After Inspector Adams left, Frank smiled; confident they had successfully tricked the police. He made a phone call to his accomplice. "The police suspect nothing and are convinced it was professionally done. Good work!"

***

Helen Randall was determined to get to the bottom of the missing items. She was suspicious of Frank Knight, but had nothing substantial in which to accuse him.

He may have the treasured articles and arranged this ploy to keep them from her, but what would he want with them? They are of no value to him. They legally belong to Mary and she could sue him out of Rockford if he did not produce them. No, there is more to this than meets the eye, she thought.

As Helen dwelled on the circumstances of the incident, the phone rang next to her in the garden. Her daughter's voice came through clearly.

"Mother, Karen. Are you definite on the Fourth of July party? That sounds like fun. What can we do to help?"

Helen had talked to Karen about the Fourth of July party, but she lied to Carl when she stormed into the house after her visit with Frank Knight. She pretended she was angry with Karen and made up a story about Karen not coming to the party. She didn't want Carl to know that the brooch and watch were missing from the safe.

"Come over some afternoon, Karen, and we'll talk about it. Come for lunch,"

They agreed on the following Wednesday at noon. Helen was surprised at Karen's tone. She wasn't always so cooperative. In fact, of her two children, Karen was the stubborn one who could be quite disagreeable at times. Helen remembered the many times Karen, as a child, disturbed the entire household because she didn't get her way.

I'm sure that girl spent more time confined to her room as punishment than most kids.

Helen found Karen even more congenial on the following Wednesday when she arrived holding a turtle cheesecake for dessert. Helen had Rose set lunch up outdoors, and in spite of the humid air, a soft breeze blew across the patio encouraging a satisfying feel for summer. Karen eyed the array of flowers.

"Mother, your flowers are beautiful."

The yellow, linen table cloth only added to the decor and no matter *whom* Helen was having for lunch, her table arrangements and surroundings had to be picture perfect, or she wasn't satisfied.

Karen's black linen suit, highlighted with a yellow scarf, was fashionably created.

Both mother and daughter would make a dress designer proud. Karen's thick crop of black hair and green eyes always assured others she looked more like her father than Peter. She also had her father's temperament.

The mother-daughter lunch was a success. Karen didn't argue, accepted advice, and Helen was agreeable. Rose had outdone herself with a dill-creamed salmon steak, sprinkled with almonds, herb rice, and a garden salad covered with a honey-mustard dressing.

"This is delicious, Rose," Karen said as Rose filled the glasses with more iced tea.

"I doubt if I'll eat much dinner tonight."

After lunch, Helen suggested they walk to the gazebo across the lawn to have some vanilla flavored coffee. "We can discuss the party's festivities there."

"Oh, I'd love that, Mother." Karen was totally cooperative and it amazed Helen.

Upon sitting at a round wicker table, Helen said, "Let's prepare our invitation list first, Karen. The Mulligan's, Kate and Don, are always so delightful at our gatherings and I like to invite them to this event."

"That's fine with me, Mother. Kate always has some interesting tale to tell."

"What about you, Karen. Is there someone in particular you'd like to add to the list?"

"Before I answer that I'm going to get a sheet of blank paper and pen from your kitchen. I think we should start writing names down and decide on how many people we should have, don't you?

"Yes, I don't want to go beyond a hundred guests, Karen. That number worked very well at our last party."

Karen stood up preparing to scoot to the kitchen, but hesitated to say, "Will you have the same caterer?"

"Gerry's did a good job at our Christmas buffet. I planned on having them again."

Preparations for the gathering went on for another hour. Karen arranged tables mentally, and made some meaningful suggestions. Helen was pleased with the outcome of their meeting.

As Karen stood in the foyer holding the door handle to leave, Helen mentioned the break-in at Frank Knight's office. She hesitated to inform the family about what was going on. She wanted to avoid too many questions about the brooch. But, perhaps Karen had heard about it and she'd share some information. Karen added very little. Only, that the police would surely find who stole them. But, an obvious flush rose from her neck to her face. Helen caught the sign.

After Karen left, Helen wondered why her daughter didn't ask how Mary was involved in all of this. Almost like she already knew, Helen thought.

* * *

Mary's pain was beginning to be more tolerable, and she was in need of less morphine each day, responding with smiles and keener conversation when Grace and Reed visited her. Grace was relieved. Several days had passed since her surgery and Nurse Albertson was coming in on a regular schedule, helping her out of bed into a nearby chair. Reed was delighted to find her sitting in a chair one afternoon when he stopped by the hospital. Stooping down and hugging her, Reed kissed her and continued to tell her day after day how much he loved her.

Grace returned to her old self again, cheerful and expectant of a better day ahead for all of them. Dr. Cherny left instructions for Mary to begin short walks down the hall. Nurse Albertson would link Mary's arm in hers, and together they would stroll as Mary dragged her IV bottle and bandaged leg. Her hair was beginning to fall softly around her ears, and she was feeling good enough to put a little makeup on in the morning. She wanted to be mentally prepared for physical therapy at the Rockford clinic.

Fourteen

*F*rank Knight's secretary looked up startled as Inspector Adams walked into the office early one morning. "If you don't mind, young lady, I would like to take another look around your boss's office. Is he in?"

"No, Sir. He usually arrives around nine o'clock."

"Do you think he'd mind if I went in there? It won't take long."

Reluctantly, she allowed it, hoping he would be in and out before Knight arrived.

However, it didn't turn out that way. Five minutes later, Frank Knight walked into his office. He looked at Nancy and she signaled with her thumb to the office, a frown on her face.

Frank crossed the threshold of the door and said, "What are you looking for, Inspector Adams?"

Carefully scrutinizing the bookshelf and safe, Adams whirled around at the sound of Knight's voice.

"Oh, Mr. Knight, I had a thought come to me last night while lying in bed, and I didn't think you'd mind my checking it out this morning," A cordial smile spread across his face.

"You certainly do get an early start," Frank said as he swung his chair around from the desk. "I do have a busy day."

"Yes, of course, I certainly will not detain you too long, but tell me again, Mr. Knight, what time was it when you left the office?"

"Around nine o'clock."

"Do you park your car out front or in the back of the building?"

"Since my office is in the front of the building, I put my car in one of the parking spaces out front."

"I noticed, Mr. Knight, that there are only four parking spaces out there."

"That's because it's a small building with only three other lawyers in it."

Frank's tone dripped with sarcasm.

"I also noticed that there is no entrance into the building from the back, so it is not likely that anyone would park back there. The fire escape is too high and practically impossible to scale for quick entry. Since your office is in the front of the building, there'd be no point in coming in the back way, would there?"

Again, Inspector Adams smiled politely as he watched Knight roll his eyes.

"See here, Adams, I'm a busy man. What are you getting at?" A flush began to creep up around Frank's collar.

"I am only inquiring, Mr. Knight, as to whether you saw any other cars in the parking lot out front when you left at nine o'clock?" Adams asked with a comfortable low speaking voice.

"There were no other cars in the parking lot when I left."

"Well, that's confusing now because Mr. Conklin, the lawyer who also has a front view office, saw the headlights of your car when you pulled out and the headlights of another car pull in. You talked with the driver in the other car, and then went on your way. When Mr. Conklin left, the other car was still in the parking lot at nine fifteen, and it was empty. Would you mind telling me who was in the other car? Since you rolled down your window and talked with the person, you must have known who it was."

Inspector Adams eyed Frank loosening his tie and perspiration forming on his brow.

The entire scene of that evening ran through Frank's mind. He had worked late purposely that evening, so he could give last minute instructions to the person in the other car. Tom Conklin told him over a coffee break that he also was working late, and that his wife was dropping him off in the morning and would pick him up around nine fifteen after her bridge game. Frank forgot all about the conversation. Tom's wife must have arrived a little earlier, around nine ten, while the other car was still in the parking space and the safe was being robbed.

Frank hesitated. Finally, he said, "A lady pulled in to ask for directions. She was lost. I talked with her a few minutes and then I left. I don't know who else pulled in or out of the parking lot after I drove off. Now, if you don't mind Inspector, I would like you to leave so I can get some work done."

Adams, suspicious of Frank's story, said, "Of course," and left.

* * *

After the Inspector left, Frank tried to settle down and figure out the next move. He was jumpy and nervous, and had no idea anyone saw him talking to the person in the other car. The excuse he gave Inspector Adams might hold. Frank's thoughts were interrupted by his secretary's intercom buzz.

Helen Randall was on the phone. "Hello, Helen"…was about as friendly as Frank would get after her threat the last time they were together.

"Why haven't you called, Frank? Surely, I have a right to know what's going on. Have the police found out anything?"

Frank detected a quivering voice on the other end of the phone asking one query after another with no semblance of connection whatsoever. Frank cringed and said, "There is nothing to report." Inspector Adams is still working on the case."

Frank expected an eruption on the other end of the phone after hearing there was nothing to report, but Helen surprised him. Calmly, she said, "Do you think Mary Bryant or Grace would know anything about the stolen pieces?"

"How could they? Mary's still in the hospital and Grace is too preoccupied with running back and forth to see her. What information could they possibly have?"

"I don't know. But it wouldn't hurt to let them know someone broke into your safe and took the items," Helen said with doubt in her voice. "After all, Frank, both those valuable items have been willed to Mary, and she should know they're gone."

"I'll think about it," answered Frank.

After hanging up, Frank became suspicious of Helen. *Why would she want Mary or even Grace involved in the burglary? Both items are willed to Mary. All it would do is add a couple more names to Inspector Adams's list. Well, why not? Maybe it would take him off of my tail.*

Fifteen

*T*he heat of July in Rockford arrived, and Grace was excited! Mary was doing so well, she would be transferred to the clinic in a couple of days. Nurse Albertson discontinued her IV, and she was walking the halls everyday with less of a limp. Dr. Cherny decided physical therapy would be the best remedy at this time to strengthen her muscles. Dr. Gordon approved and decided to test her mental capabilities before moving her to the Sports Clinic.

He walked into Mary's room just short of dinner time one late afternoon. Mary looked up from her letter writing when she heard the tap on her door. She smiled when Dr. Gordon took her hand in his.

"How are you doing today, pretty lady?"

"Much better, Doctor! And it's a pleasure to say that."

"Do you have any questions about your transfer over to the Sports Clinic?"

"I think only one. How long would I be there?

"Well, you know it depends on how well you respond. The usual length of time is about twenty days, but it could be sooner."

"Will I be able to go home after the twenty days?"

"Most likely you will return to the hospital for a day or two to be checked out, both mentally and physically. If everything is fine, then we'll sign you out."

"That sounds good to me, Doctor."

Doctor Gordon waved goodbye to Mary as he turned to leave. He had no doubt she was ready for the routine procedures at the Clinic.

* * *

Monday morning, while Reed chaired his normal personnel meeting at the newspaper, an ambulance pulled up at the emergency entrance of the hospital to take Mary to Rockford Clinic to start her physical therapy treatment. Rockford Clinic was in another newly constructed building a short distance from the hospital. As mentioned earlier by her doctor, she could possibly be there twenty days. Nurse Albertson buzzed around her room, collecting her belongings and instructing the nurses' aides in preparing Mary for her transfer. Floral bouquets were gathered and placed on a cart along with books, plants and magazines; all of which would join Mary in her ride to the Clinic. Mary smiled and waved as she was pushed down the hall to the elevator, grateful to have all of the past weeks behind her.

It wasn't long before she went from one painful experience to another at the Sports Center. Therapy was hard, strenuous and long. Her body hurt beyond comprehension. Day after day, therapists wheeled Mary to the equipment room, returning her an hour later completely exhausted. Her disposition with Reed and Grace changed from cheerful to cranky and irritable. Both tried very hard to understand, but sometimes, because of the intense pain, Mary was nasty, demanding, and insulting; causing Reed to visit less often. Grace began to worry about this. She loved Reed and didn't want Mary to lose him, knowing quite well that she was not her normal self. The pain of therapy was more than she could bear.

Some mornings Reed visited her before going to work and he'd stop at the Clinic to give her a hug or peck on the cheek. Early morning being her most painful time, she would bite at him with, "Why are you here so early? There's nothing to tell. Even Dr. Cherny hasn't been here yet." Dr. Cherny stopped in to see Mary's progress every morning on his regular scheduled visits.

Reed would try to comfort her with understanding words. "Just thought a hug would get us both off to a good start this morning!"

"HUG?" Mary questioned sarcastically. "I can't even move and you want to hug."

Reed just squeezed her hand and left.

Grace had even more of her irony than Reed.

"Take that robe back home. I don't like it. It's too restricting. I told you I wanted a white terry cloth." And again, "Can't you find a scuff-type slipper that I can just slip into?" Or at another time, "Come back tomorrow, I hurt too much to talk today."

Reed, desperate from her abrasive attitude, talked to Susie about it one day.

"Why don't you send her love notes every day? Drop them off at the Clinic or mail them. Trust me, she won't yell at the delivery fellow."

Reed took Susie's advice and sent short "I love you" notes every day. Some he mailed and some he simply dropped off on his way to work, asking that the letters be delivered by the mail boy.

Mary would read them and cry. Nurse Albertson put them in a square cloth-covered box on her nightstand, so she could re-read them often as a means of comfort and calm for Mary's worse days.

Grace, on the other hand, brought small bouquets a couple times a week that she bought from a nearby florist. She'd arranged them beautifully in the vases in Mary's room. Occasionally, she would even buy little cheery gifts in the hospital gift shop to brighten her day.

This went on for two weeks until finally, after repeated lifting and bending, the pain was beginning to lessen. It was important that the leg be straight and muscles strong before Mary could begin on her own strength. Each day, with a therapist beside her, she would walk a path outside the Clinic slowly, determined to overcome the hand life had dealt her and walk unassisted. Mary knew there was talk between the doctors about a lesser surgery on the other leg. Time would tell if this had to be done. She couldn't help thinking that progress now might eliminate another surgery.

Mary's time at the Center began to take a toll on Grace, and she longed for the day when her daughter could finally come home. Reed would be picking her up later for an afternoon visit at the Clinic. She arose and went into Mary's room to clean it from top to bottom with the hope her energy would create a force that would accelerate Mary's return. The phone rang while she was stripping the bed.

"Hello," she answered cheerfully, then glanced at the clock on the nightstand next to Mary's bed which read nine o'clock.

"This is Frank Knight, Mrs. Bryant." His strong voice caught her attention immediately.

"Yes, Mr. Knight, how are you?"

"Doing fairly well, but we have a problem." His voice dropped, giving Grace the impression that the news wasn't good. "The brooch and Rolex watch are gone."

Grace hesitated and simply repeated, "Gone?"

After Frank told Grace about the whole incident, he asked if he would be able to speak to Mary.

"Since these items have been willed to her, it's important she know what has taken place,"

"She's been transferred to the Sports Center, Mr. Knight. I'll see her this afternoon, and pass on your message."

On their way to the Clinic, Grace related the whole story to Reed. He listened, while he drove, but didn't say a word. After pulling into a parking space under a shaded tree, he turned off the engine and turned to Grace.

"Let me get this straight. A burglar broke into Frank Knight's safe and stole these two items, and there is no evidence. Now, because there is no sign of the safe being damaged in any way, the police are convinced it was done professionally. Is that right?"

Grace nodded. "And, Frank Knight wants to talk to Mary. He thinks that since these items officially belong to Mary, she should know what has happened," said Grace as she grabbed hold of the door handle, intending to open it.

Reed jumped out of the car, walked around and opened the door for her, saying as he helped her out of the car. "There's reason for some serious thought here. It just doesn't add up. Someone had to know those items were in Frank Knight's safe. They also had to know the combination. Who do you think that could be?"

* * *

Mary looked great as they walked into the large equipment room where she was rotating her legs on a small bicycle. She wore a pink sports suit that Grace bought while shopping with her neighbor. One of the aides in the clinic placed a ruffled purple collar around her neck which accentuated her sparkling blue eyes. Her auburn hair, shoulder length now, curled around her forehead making her appearance picture perfect. Reed stared in awe at her beauty as he bent down to kiss her. Grace gave her a hug.

She was progressing nicely and responding to her doctor's satisfaction. What a difference a couple weeks made! She could see results now, and made up her mind to get her body back again. Yes, she limped a bit, and yes, she walked slower, but that would all end with consistency and determination.

The Sports Clinic had wheelchairs for athletes, who were hurt badly, lined up behind some tables. Aides roamed through the Clinic and one of them suggested Reed use one of the wheelchairs to take Mary out to the courtyard for some fresh air. Grace and Reed did this often when they visited to keep her from getting tired, especially after her long hours of exercising.

They went out to the benches in the courtyard today, where the sky's shade of baby blue looked rich and inviting, Mary loved the feel of the hot sun on her arms. Reed parked her chair in the sunlight, while he and Grace sat on a shady bench, surrounded by honeysuckle bushes. Grace repeated Frank Knight's story about the stolen articles to Mary.

"So, you told him I would call him?" asked Mary.

"No, I told him I'd pass on his message."

"Hmmm, what do you think I should do, Reed?"

"I think you should get a lawyer, Mary. I can recommend a good one. Stay out of it, and let your lawyer call Frank Knight."

"Will you gave me his name and telephone number, Reed. I'll call him later."

"Michael Bromley is his name. Just a

minute, I think I have his card in my wallet."

Reed found the lawyer's card and gave it to Mary. She called him after Reed and Grace left.

* * *

"Mr. Bromley, this is Mary Clark. I'm in need of an attorney's advice, and Reed Lowell has given me your card. I'm at a Sports Clinic right now with injuries from an automobile accident, but do you think we could arrange a meeting to discuss the problem."

"I know the Sports Clinic very well, Miss Clark. I spent some time there myself after a leg injury playing basketball. I could come over to the Clinic tomorrow morning if you have some free time during the morning hours."

"I am usually finished with my morning routine about ten. Could you make it ten-thirty, allowing me time to shower?"

"Yes, that would work out fine. Let me ask you, Miss Clark, what sort of advice do you need?"

"Please call me Mary. It concerns a will that my ex-husband left after he was killed in a skiing accident."

"That's all the information I need right now. You can give me the details tomorrow."

"Thank you, Mr. Bromley."

The following morning, Grace called Mary to say she'd visit her in the afternoon since she had a hair appointment in the morning. Mary informed her that she and Michael Bromley would be meeting at ten thirty. "Take your time, Mother; I'll be tied up with the attorney until after lunch."

Reed also checked in and Mary gave him the same message. "You're busy, Reed. Why don't you plan on coming after dinner, and I'll tell you all about my conversation with Michael Bromley."

Her attorney arrived right on time. Mary gave him all the information he needed, such as, when she married Peter Clark, when they divorced, when she gave Peter the watch, and when she gave the brooch back to Peter after their divorce. But, explaining the burglary appeared to be more difficult because she didn't have all the details. She informed him of Helen Randall's visit to see her, and how she suspected it could very possibly be Helen who had something to do with the robbery.

"I understand that the police have put an Inspector Adams on the case. I don't have any information on him."

"I can get that from the police, "answered Michael.

She answered Michael's questions as best she could and after Mary mentioned that

Frank Knight was Peter's attorney, he decided to contact Frank on his own.

Michael Bromley documented all the information Mary gave him, then said, "This is plenty to go on, Mary. I will get back to you as soon as I can."

* * *

Frank Knight's office phone rang early Monday morning.

"Frank Knight here,"

"Mr. Knight, I'm Michael Bromley, Mary Clark's lawyer. I wonder if I could take a few minutes of your time to ask some questions."

"Oh, Mr. Bromley, I didn't know Mary hired a lawyer. I would rather speak to her before talking to a lawyer. But, since you've called how can I help?"

This was a surprised call for Frank. He had to be very careful about what he said. When Michael asked him where his office was located, Frank spoke cautiously.

"Our office is on the same street as Memorial Hospital, only we are on the South end of Rockton. The address is 485," answered Frank.

"You said "our." Do you share the office with another?"

Frank hesitated, annoyed with himself for using the word "our."

"Yes, it's a new building and I share it with another lawyer."

Michael kept the conversation friendly by saying that's prime location. It's close to restaurants and shopping, etc. But the digression threw Frank off, and when Michael said, "I have a lawyer friend in that vicinity. I haven't seen him in a while and wonder if he's sharing the office with you. Can you tell me his name?"

That staggered Frank. He didn't want to give him Tom Conklin's name for fear Tom would tell him he saw Frank talking to someone in another car the night of the burglary. Knowing Michael Bromley would contact Tom, he hesitated for a moment.

"What's your friend's name?" asked Frank.

"Tim Barry. We went through law school together."

"Frank smiled and said, "Sorry, that's not him."

Before hanging up, Michael asked, "What have the police done to find the suspect and who's in charge?

Frank did his best to avoid mentioning Inspector Adams, but had no choice. "I received a call from the Police Department telling me an Inspector Bud Adams has been assigned to the case." He loosened his tie and breathed a sigh of relief after the conversation ended.

Michael contacted Helen Randall first. She assured him she knew nothing about the burglary and turned him over to Clifford Lakes, her lawyer. He decided to hold off on calling Inspector Adams, preferring to call Clifford Lakes instead.

"Mary returned the brooch to Peter Clark, indicating she didn't want it. Therefore, it rightfully belongs in the family," said Clifford Lakes to Michael.

"Sorry," said Michael, "That won't cut the mustard. Peter gave it back to Mary in his will. The will has the final word and unless Mary willingly gives it to Helen Randall, it belongs to her."

"Well," said Clifford Lakes. "It may turn out that no one gets the brooch except the perpetrator. We may never see either item again."

"Don't count on it. I'm sure I'll be talking to you in time." The conversation ended.

While Michael drove back to his office, he thought the whole scenario was a set-up. *Clifford Lakes, you're wrong. We **will** see those items again.*

* * *

Frank Knight looked at the clock on the mantel when the phone rang. It was eleven o'clock. Kathryn had retired for the night so he hurried to answer it.

"Hello."

A low-pitched voice said, "Are you aware that the police suspect you of planning the robbery."

Frank was taken back. "Why are you calling here again?" he asked sharply.

"Because, Frank, this isn't going away. Inspector Adams and Mary's lawyer are asking too many questions, and I'm afraid they will get around to me."

"What kind of questions?"

"Someone saw you talking to a woman in a car in front of your office. That *someone* was me, Frank," the voice said anxiously.

"They don't know that. I told Inspector Adams it was someone asking for directions," whispered Frank, swiping his forehead with a shaky hand. "I wish you wouldn't call me here. My wife is going to get suspicious."

"I don't give a damn about your wife, Frank. You knew I wanted that brooch in the worst way, and you concocted this whole scheme. It's not going well. Not like you said it would. Your eyes only saw the dollar signs that I would pay to have that brooch. Do you remember saying that Frank? Everyone would think it was gone, and after a while stop thinking about it.' What was the other thing you said, Frank? 'Mary didn't want it. She wouldn't care if it had been stolen."

"Why don't you get out of town for a while?" suggested Frank. "Let the whole thing blow over. Take the items with you. If they can't find them, they will eventually come to the conclusion they're gone. Just be careful you keep them well guarded. Carry them on your body at all times and definitely avoid suitcases or drawers. Put them under your pillow at night. When you get to where you are going, call me at my office, never here, okay? Goodbye!"

Frank hung up.

* * *

As Mary progressed from walking to running on the clinic treadmill, Dr. Cherny realized that her change in behavior needed a change in surroundings. He walked into her room after lunch one afternoon. Mary was sitting at a round table. She looked up and smiled.

"Dr. Cherny, what a nice surprise."

"Hi Mary, you were told early in the game that you would be here about twenty days. You are doing well, but Dr. Gordon and I thought it best for you to stay a bit longer. A little more mending is needed. But, we thought you deserved a reward."

Sarcastically, Mary answered, "Oh, do I get to have a glass of wine with dinner, or maybe more chocolate?" She had been counting the days and didn't want to stay any longer.

"Well, no. You haven't been that good. How do you feel about going home for a couple of days?"

She brightened, but then asked, "How much longer do I have to stay here?"

"We think a full month of therapy would work the best. We're concerned about that limp you have. We are also thinking that exercise and therapy might correct the other leg, and we won't have to operate on it. If you were thinking twenty days, well we are talking only ten days more. You can do that, Mary."

Dr. Cherny convinced Mary to return after a few days home. She left on a balmy, warm Thursday in July with instructions to return on the follow Monday. Nurse Albertson was ordered to keep a close eye on her, and she visited Mary at her home on Saturday morning. After her visit, she made her report in Mary's file.

Not only did the decision lift her spirits, but it helped repair the cracks in her relationship with Reed. Her excitement on the phone, after Dr. Cherney left, was contagious for both Reed and Grace, even though a bit of sadness crept into the conversation when they learned she had to return to the Clinic for more therapy.

After picking her up, Reed cheered as he carried her over Grace's threshold, and Grace beamed with a tearful smile.

Thursday evening at home, Mary asked for her favorite pork roast dinner and a bottle of Pinot Grigio wine that Grace picked up at the liquor store that morning and chilled all afternoon. The purple New Guinea impatiens overlapping the path leading to the willow tree seemed to sparkle as Mary held Reed's arm strolling carefully to the lawn furniture. Reed protected her every move. When she reached for a magazine on a side table, he jumped to retrieve it for her. He made sure her wine glass was filled.

Grace had prepared a plate of appetizers that he carefully carried out and placed close to Mary. In addition to all of this attention, he lifted and carried her to the dinner table. Laughter filled the air. The time spent together was exactly what they needed to strengthen them for the underlying possibility that Mary may have to have a second surgery.

* * *

After Mary's returned to the Clinic, a consultation was held between the two doctors while she continued her therapy for ten more days. Several x-rays were taken of her other leg, and researched over and over again. As hard as they tried to eliminate another surgery, it was decided that the knee was damaged too much and needed some replacement.

The second surgery, scheduled for Tuesday August 6 at 8:00, came quickly. Again, Reed joined Grace at the hospital, but this time holding hands as their anxiety levels soared. After getting Mary's signature on the necessary surgery forms, the orderly greeted them in the waiting. Then the wait!

The pre-operative x-rays were taken the day before showing Dr. Cherny the necessary paths to take to correct the leg. He determined the second leg surgery would not be as severe as the first, and should take less time to repair. Most of the work would be done on the knee that banged against the steering wheel when she was thrown against the door.

This morning, two nurses came in washed and shaved the leg and knee. Nurse Albertson checked her vital signs; pulse and blood pressure. Since the hospital had all of her past medical records, consisting of her medications and possible allergies, surgery would proceed without delay.

Reed and Grace were allowed to see her for a few moments before she was taken into the operating room. After a last-minute hug and quick kiss from Reed and Grace, she was pushed through swinging doors that closed behind, leaving her best friend and lover worried and desperate once more. This time, though, the wait was shorter.

* * *

At ten-thirty, Reed held the cafeteria door for Grace as she collected her belongings from the small booth where the sunlight dried the tears on her cheeks. The hot coffee and donut helped a lot to calm the jitters in her stomach. They strolled down the hall and again Reed reached for her hand. He felt it comforting and hoped the contact gave Grace some strength.

To their surprise, they found Dr. Cherny looking for them in the waiting room.

"There you are," he said removing his surgical cap from his head. "All looks very good. At first, we considered a knob-type replacement in the knee, but decided against it after seeing there were no cracked bones. She only needed debris removed and torn cartilage repaired." Smiling a bit, he followed with, "If she obeys the doctor's orders, she'll be good as new before you know it." He shook hands with Reed, nodded to Grace and left. As they turned to each other slightly dazed from the whole quick report, Dr. Cherny returned saying, "Oh, she's in Intensive Care. Give her a half hour, but just stay a short while."

Greatly relieved, the pair returned to their seats. Reed picked up the newspaper lying on the table and Grace flipped through a magazine, wishing the time away.

Sixteen

*A*ll thoughts of Cheryl Cunningham's wedding, scheduled for September, had been erased. Reed had moved on and refused to even think about his former fiancé. Phoebe brought the subject up once and Reed cut her off with, "Don't even mention it, Mother."

Mary's healing time at the Clinic went from bad to better in a short length of time. Each therapy exercise made her more determined to get past this whole horrible experience. She wanted her life back again.

The day finally arrived for Mary to return home. Grace was thrilled. Even Mary's slight limp and slow movements, that worried her in the beginning, became unnoticeable after a short period of time and didn't bother her at all. She was amazed that Mary's knee replacement gave her very little discomfort.

Once a week, mostly on a late Saturday afternoon, she prepared a special dinner for Reed and Mary to be enjoyed with wine next to the willow tree. September breezes were still enjoyed on occasions before the cold winter months arrived.

Although the knee didn't bother Mary, her slight limp and slow movements did. Opening her bedroom window before retiring one evening, she watched the organdy curtains sway and blow in almost a musical way in the September breezes. I have got to help myself, she thought as she watched the moonlight drift across the ceiling of her room.

The following morning temperatures dropped and cold temperatures found Mary shimmering under a light blanket. She slipped out of bed and closed the window. As she looked out at the cloudy morning, she made a decision.

Grace found her rummaging through her closet. "What are you doing? I put your cup out for some hot coffee."

"No hot coffee this morning, Mother. I have a mission in mind. Where are the sweats I always fall back on when the weather gets cold? I found my earmuffs and gloves, but I need those old tennis shoes. You know, Mother, the ones I would paint in."

"Where are you going, Mary?"

She remembered Reed's remark in the hospital when she cried with depression, "I'm going to start out walking before I run and I'll need to keep warm."

Mary followed her mother to the attic

where old clothes were stored in a big trunk, and to her surprise, even the old tennis shoes were there. She smiled thinking, *Mother never throws anything away.*

Bundled up with a hooded sweat shirt over earmuffs, Mary stood on the front porch wondering if she really wanted to attempt this. She saw Grace peeking out the front window with frightened eyes as she began to walk slowly down the path toward an open road. The large farmland lay before her as she eyed the tired willow tree brushing its branches on the ground that would turn brown soon with the colder weather coming on. She thought about the second surgery as she limped down the gravel path. She had been blessed with healing that, at times, she thought would never come. A few tiny tears gathered in the corner of her eyes as she made her way to the main road, tears of happiness for Reed's love. Something else she never counted on. She hugged the side of the road as trucks and wagons went by.

The next morning Mary bundled up again just as the morning light appeared, and stood on her front porch ready to go. She had walked one mile the morning before and found herself tired and sore. This is not going to deter me, she thought. For one week, she walked only a mile. Only Grace and the therapist knew what she was doing.

She decided not to tell Reed just yet. The therapist instructed her to tread lightly, don't push. Listen to your body. When you hear it say stop, stop and come home.

It took two months before Mary could go beyond one mile. Her goal, at first, was always to the Anderson's mailbox, the neighbor down the road. When she'd make that she'd turn around to return home. But she passed the Anderson's mailbox on October 2$^{nd.}$ By this time, Mary had achieved two miles easily. Her excitement was beyond words. Dr. Cherney stood dumbfounded when he discovered Mary's limp was gone. The therapist hugged her. And Grace's frightened eyes dissolved into a bright smile as she watched Mary begin her walk each morning. The secret of her gains was revealed when Reed noticed the changes in her.

Prompted by the huge amounts of snow in November piled high along the nearby roads, Mary joined a YWCA where she could avoid bundling up in heavy clothing because of the cold. The "Y" had an enclosed running track and not far from home. Again, she was grateful for Grace's frugal ways as she dragged an old bicycle from the garage. She remembered the Christmas morning it stood bright and shinning next to the tree. She was twelve years old. Her mother and dad smiled from ear to ear as they looked at her surprised expression. She loved this bike even though the years covered it with rust and age now.

"How are you getting to the "Y" Mary? Reed asked after he heard her plans.

"I'm going to ride my old bike. I'll wait until the city clears the roads in the morning." The fresh air will be invigorating.

Seventeen

*I*t spite of the passing of time, the stolen brooch and Rolex watch remained in the limelight. Inspector Adams's call after Mary returned home from the "Y" made it obvious to her that he needed more evidence.

"Good Morning, Miss Bryant. I wonder if I could have a few words with you this morning about the recent burglary in Frank Knight's office."

"I don't know if I can help much, Inspector, but I'll try. Would ten o'clock be okay for you?"

"That would work out fine."

Mary's doorbell rang exactly at ten on a windy morning. Trees swayed and beat against the living room window announcing a possible rain. Mary opened the front door to let Inspector Adams in. She liked the gentle warmth of him, the suntanned face with a few winkles around his eyes, and his broad grin with even white teeth.

"Come in, Inspector."

Mary led him into the living room,

pointed to the paisley couch, and asked him to sit down.

"Can I get you a cup of coffee?"

"No, thank you, I just had breakfast."

"How can I help you?" asked Mary slowly slipping into the chair across from him.

"Miss Bryant, I feel this is a perfectly planned setup between two people but it lacks necessary evidence before they can be caught."

"Do you have any idea who the two culprits are?"

"Well, I have my suspicions, and I'm trying to eliminate the innocent ones. Can I ask you a couple of questions?"

"I've really put all of this in my lawyer's hands, Inspector. I'm not so sure I can answer any of your questions. Furthermore, I was in the Clinic when the burglary occurred. What could I possibly know about it? My lawyer was supposed to call you."

"Your lawyer has called me, Miss Bryant, but I wanted to talk to you personally. I hope that's all right. I'd like to ask you about your employer, Mr. Lowell, and your mother. Did they spend most of their time with you?"

"Inspector, my mother would be your least suspicious person. She was too busy worrying about me. As far as Mr. Lowell is concerned, he runs a reputable newspaper and neglected his business interests because he was concerned about me."

"As I said earlier, Miss Bryant, I'm trying to eliminate the innocent ones.

I've been filled in on the details about your marriage to Peter Randall, the will, the brooch and the watch, but I need more evidence. How well do you know Frank Knight?"

"I don't know him at all. He called me to set up an appointment to go over the will. Right after that, I had the accident and most of his contacts were with my mother. While I was in the Clinic, he called my mother asking to speak to me. It was then I called my lawyer. I'm afraid, Inspector, you will have to get further information from him."

Inspector Adams knew he overstepped the line by asking about Frank Knight. He had his suspicions about Frank, and thought Mary might reveal more. But, he decided to just thank her and leave.

Mary leaned against the closed door after the Inspector left and heaved a sigh. With the burglary still on her mind, she opened her mother's bedroom door and found her napping.

Not wanting to disturb her, she decided on a cup of tea and went into the kitchen. As she sat sipping the hot tea slowly, she began to think further on the robbery. *The Rolex watch is not the important item in this burglary, but the brooch is. Both items had* to be taken to make it look like a routine burglary. The real question is who would want that expensive brooch bad enough to steal it? Mary could only think of one person, Helen Randall. She knew Helen would go to any lengths to get what she wanted. Mary's lawyer had convinced her that the brooch was legally hers and Helen could not obtain it without Mary's permission. So Helen had to find another way.

She poured another cup of tea and picked up a chocolate chip cookie off a tray Grace had sitting on the kitchen table. She began to go a step further in her thinking.

Inspector Adams suspected two people. Who would help Helen steal the brooch? She doesn't drive, so she had to have an accomplice. Who would be brave or bold enough to sneak into Frank Knight's office, know the safe code number, and steal the two items?

And, how did that person get the code number? It seems probable that more than two people are involved. Mary pushed away from the table, put her hand to her heart and said out loud, "I think I know who would help Helen with this robbery."

Her first thought was to call Reed and run all of this by him, but before she got to the phone, Grace came out of the bedroom.

"Mother, I've got a few things to tell you

and Reed. I'm phoning him to come over this evening and I'll tell you two all about it. In the meantime, I've got an errand to run. I drove the car yesterday without any problems and I can do it again today."

Since Mary's car was totaled in the accident. Reed had loaned her a Dodge Dart his father bought him before he died. She remembered their conversation, *Mary, forget the bike. I have this car sitting in my garage not being used. It's at your disposal. Use it until something better comes along.*

Reed had thought about selling it many times, but memories of his father had kept him from doing that. He had also enjoyed taking it out for a spin occasionally.

Since the car was a stick shift Mary worried about driving it at first. Her knee was not completely healed and switching gears might cause problems. But evidently her exercises helped cure some of the pain in her knee and she drove the Dart without any problems.

With that, Mary dialed Reed's number while Grace stood listening and wondering, "What's she up to now?"

* * *

Reed arrived around seven thirty that evening. A cold wind swept through Rockford blowing leaves and debris all around as he stepped out of the car. He made a mad dash for the door and Mary let him in. He pulled her close, kissing her gently on the lips.

"Come in the kitchen, Reed. It's getting colder out there and I thought a cup of hot chocolate would be a good idea, or would you like something stronger?"

"I think the hot chocolate will hit the spot."

Grace had pulled a warm peach cobbler from the oven. She looked up, smiled at Reed and set the pan on a board to cool.

Reed sat on a kitchen chair. His long legs stretched in front of him.

"What's going on, Mary?

"Plenty!" she answered as she poured hot chocolate into three mugs.

Grace distributed three pieces of cobbler around the table along with forks and napkins before sitting down.

Mary took a deep breath and began her report.

"I rode over to the office this afternoon to see your secretary, Susie. She and Karen, Helen Randall's daughter, have become good friends. I led Susie to believe that I had come to pick up a few files that needed my attention because before long, I would be coming back to work. I wanted her to think I needed a head start on some backlogged work. We talked about a lot of things before

Susie mentioned Karen."

"By the way, Mary, have you seen Karen Clark lately?

"No, Susie, I have very little contact with Karen or her mother since Peter and I divorced. You seem concerned. Is she all right?"

"I called her to set up a date for a lunch, and her maid said she was out-of-town, and she had no idea when she'd be back. The maid's comment that they had no idea when she'd be back concerned me. The last time I saw her, she mentioned a trip they were planning to Boston, and taking their kids."

Mary explained all this to Reed and Grace, even mentioning that Susie had called Karen two days after she heard about the burglary. Then, she continued to say that Susie had received a call from Karen a couple of days before, letting her know she was back in Rockford. When Susie asked her where she went, Karen said to visit a sick friend in Wisconsin. They chatted awhile and then Susie asked her if anything new had developed on the stolen items. Her reply was, "No, whoever did that got away with it. That beautiful brooch is gone. My mother is very upset about it."

"So, what's all this prove, Mary?" asked Reed.

"Not much now, but I remember the day Peter gave me the brooch as if it were yesterday. Helen objected and Karen was livid. Karen wanted that brooch in the worst way. I am convinced that the two of them have worked together to steal the brooch so that I don't get it back. Karen is suspect."

"Do you think she would go to such lengths of stealing to get the brooch?"

"Yes, I do, Mother."

"And" said Reed, "What happened to the trip to Boston?"

"That's another thing," Mary answered. "Why the lie?"

Reed walked to the board on top of the stove to get another piece of cobbler. As he cut, he said, "If Karen or Helen are involved in the burglary, it's really too bad since you may have just given the brooch back. Do you think you might have done that, Mary? Or, do you really want it?"

"No, I have no use for it. I don't want anything to remind me of Peter. I'm sorry he died, but he's a part of my life, I want to forget. You are right. They could have had the brooch without a criminal way of getting it. What bothers me the most is that an ordinary burglar would not have known the safe code, or even where the safe was located behind the books. Even Frank Knight can be guilty of giving the code to the perpetrator. There are a lot of unanswered questions."

"You're right," said Reed.

Mary continued. "I'm consulting with you two because I'm not quite sure whether it's a good idea to tell Inspector Adams or Michael Bromley about all of this."

Mary stopped talking and glanced back and forth at the two of them, hoping for some advice.

Reed sat up straight, put his elbow on the table holding his chin in his hand and just stared at her. Grace sat in shocked silence.

Reed took a few moments to think and then said, "Call, Michael, Mary! Give him your theory on all of this. Let him handle the Inspector."

Another half-hour went by as the threesome batted ideas back and forth until Grace glanced at the kitchen wall clock. "Ten o'clock, I'm going to bed."

Eighteen

*W*hile Mary speculated further on her hunches, Inspector Adams decided to again visit Tom Conklin, the lawyer who said he saw Knight talking to a woman in a car. Tom knew cars well, and when Inspector Adams asked him if he recognized the make of the car the woman was driving, Tom said, "black, 1968 Chevy Malibu. You know, Inspector, I remember writing that license number down. I do that without realizing it sometimes, but now I can't remember where I put it."

Frank felt a quick adrenalin flush. He could check the owner out in a minute, especially since he knew the make of the car. No luck though, Tom couldn't locate the license plate number. On his way out of the office he said, "I'll leave my card. Call me when you find it. It's important."

Since he had something of a lead to go on with the make of the car, he decided to check the cars of Frank's close clients, the Randall Family for instance. If the brooch was so valuable, he wondered how the children from the first marriage felt about

Peter giving the brooch to Mary.

Frank's secretary helped more than she realized when she gave Adams a few telephone numbers. He had phoned her saying he needed to talk to some people regarding the burglary, and she offered the numbers willingly.

When Adams phoned Karen, she wasn't available, so he dialed Helen Randall's number. She answered the phone.

"Mrs. Randall, this is Inspector Adams of the Rockford Police Department. I wondered if I could come over and have a few words with you concerning the robbery at Frank Knight's office."

Helen agreed and twenty minutes later Adams was sitting in Helen Randall's parlor. He was glad to get indoors since the weather had turned damp and cold. He cleared his throat and began, "I won't take up too much of your time. Just need a few items cleared up in my mind."

Helen said nothing. Carl looked in as he walked past the parlor entrance, and at first, she hesitated to introduce him to Inspector Adams. But, she did so reluctantly.

"Nice to meet you, Inspector," responded Carl as he extended his hand. The two men shook hands before Carl turned his attention back to his wife. "Helen, I'm taking my car in for a checkup and should be back within an hour."

Helen nodded her approval.

"Cars, somehow, they always need attention, don't they?" Adams said haphazardly.

"I suppose," she replied.

"What kind do you have, Mrs. Randall?' asked Adams.

"We have a Cadillac, Inspector, but I don't drive. Our chauffeur takes me out when I need to go somewhere. Now, Inspector, what items do you want cleared up?"

He thought a moment and said, "Can you give me a description of the items stolen, Mrs. Randall? You were very familiar with the brooch, and I thought you, of all people, could describe it to me thoroughly."

Helen spoke up immediately, "I can describe the brooch perfectly, but the watch was a gift from Mary to Peter, and I only saw it once or twice on Peter's wrist. I remember it being a Rolex and having a diamond on each side of the time face, but other than that it was just a normal man's watch. The brooch, on the other hand," she said covetously, "was a gorgeous piece of work."

The desire in Helen's voice and her longing to possess the brooch made it obvious how much she wanted it. She described the raised mother-of-pearl woman's head embossed on a salmon colored background, and told how it was surrounded with twenty-four diamonds. It not only could be worn as a brooch but it could be placed on a silver chain, if desired. "It is exquisite, the most beautiful cameo you have ever seen. It had been in our family for years and never should have been given to Mary Bryant. And Inspector, it should be mine." Looking directly into Adams eyes she said, "I would give my eye teeth to have it, but I didn't steal it."

"Did any member of the family object to Peter giving it to Mary?"

"I'm not sure, Inspector. My daughter could have been upset about it, but she never mentioned it to me."

"Did you have someone else steal it for you, Mrs. Randall?"

Helen was horrified at his question. "No, Inspector Adams, I did not. How dare you imply such an idea! That brooch belongs in our family, but I would not stoop so low. Furthermore, Mary Bryant doesn't even want it. The law is the law, Inspector, but if that brooch is ever located, I will continue to demand it back through the courts."

Adams bowed out gracefully and left. He was convinced Helen was innocent, but someone wanted that brooch bad enough to steal it. He needed more evidence, more proof, as to who the culprit was before confirming his conclusions. When Helen

Randall had mentioned her daughter might have been upset about it, it rang a bell in the Inspector's head. He decided to do some research on another member of the family.

***

Several thoughts had roamed through Carl's mind while he drove over to the car dealership. *Did Helen say "Inspector?" Did she mean police inspector? If so, what would she have to do with a police inspector? I better ask some questions when I get home.*

When he returned home after Inspector Adams left, he found Helen pruning a hawthorn bush in the backyard. As she snipped and shaped the bush, he stood for a moment watching her.

"Helen?" As he said her name, she jumped and turned.

"Oh, you frightened me I didn't expect you back so soon."

"I'm sorry I did that, but I have a question. Did you call that man who was here earlier "Inspector? Is he a police inspector?"

Helen cringed. She was silent for a moment. *Oh dear, what will I tell him?*

She really didn't want Carl involved in any of this, but she would have to tell him some of the truth. He would have to know it all eventually anyway.

"Yes Carl, he's a police inspector. There has been a break-in at Frank Knight's office and two valuable items were stolen from his safe."

"What's that got to do with you?"

"One was my mother's expensive brooch and the other a Rolex watch."

"Your mother's brooch? Why would Frank Knight have that valuable piece of jewelry in his safe?"

"Let's go in and have a cup of tea, Carl, and I'll tell you the whole story."

Helen removed her garden gloves and took Carl's hand as they strolled back into the house.

After she gave Carl the details of events pertaining to the burglary, he was stunned that all this was going on and he didn't know it.

"Does this Inspector Adams suspect you?"

"No. I don't think so. He just wanted me to give him a description of the brooch.

I wasn't much help on the Rolex watch because I never really got a good look at it. Mary Bryant gave it to Peter as a gift. Both items belong to her. Frank Knight, being Peter's lawyer, gained possession of them since they were in Peter's will."

Carl pushed away from the kitchen table and stood up. "You know, Helen I was in

Frank Knight's office a few times in my earlier years before I met you, and at one time, he went into the safe to get some important papers out while I was there. I could tell the code had several numbers to it. It wasn't something you could just guess at. How did anyone get into that safe without knowing the code? This is suspicious and either Frank or someone close to Frank is the guilty party."

When Carl walked out the back door to the patio, Helen breathed a sigh of relief. She thought sure he'd want to get involved and cause more of a conflict than they already had.

* * *

In the meantime, Adams returned to his office. As he pulled his desk chair out, the phone rang.

"Inspector Adams, this is Officer Sloan."

"Yes Sloan. How are you?"

"Fine, Sir. But, thought you might like to know that I found a black button while dusting for fingerprints in Frank Knight's office. I thought you might like to see it. I've put it in a small manila envelope in your middle desk drawer. It might belong to the burglar."

"Thanks for telling me. I just walked in my office. I'll look at it."

After hanging up, Adams pulled his desk drawer open and took out the envelope. Cupping his left hand, he dropped the button into it from the envelope. The button was small, covered with black satin and showed remains of black threads which led Adams to think it could have come from a woman's blouse or glove.

The threads were broken indicating the button could have been torn from its intended article. The Inspector thought deeply and decided to take it to Myron Cooke for a professional opinion and see if fingerprints were available. Buttoning a glove could indeed produce fingerprints.

* * *

Myron Cooke was Director of Research in the Rockford Police Department. He was the man to see for thorough lab work on fingerprints or blood analysis. Six feet, seven inches tall, thin, gangly and pre-occupied at all times, was the best description of him, and when he zeroed in on a case, there was no telling what he could come up with.

Inspector Adams knocked on the door and entered. Half glasses on his nose, Myron looked up to see who was invading his privacy. He could be very selfish about his privacy. But, seeing Adams, he relented because he truly loved the man. Myron, in his own secret way, scrutinized people scrupulously knowing a good one from a not-so-good one and in his opinion Adams was truly a good one.

"My friend," he said. "How are you? Where've you been? It's been awhile since you've knocked at my door."

Inspector Adams smiled and extended his hand. "I've missed you," he said.

"And I you," said Myron. "What's going on?"

"Well, I've got this little button that might help me solve a mystery. Do you think you can help? I've come to the best source," said Adams.

Myron, sitting at his lab desk, waited with an adrenalin surge as Adams released the button from the manila envelope onto a paper towel.

"Ah! How lovely, black satin one of my favorites! My late wife wore black satin often. Oh, how I miss her."

Adams smiled and waited while Myron put gloves on before placing the button on the glass slab of his microscope to search for fingerprints.

"Yes," he said in deep thought. "There's a bit of a print. We'll check it out and get back to you. Myron placed his glasses back on the tip of his nose, looked up at the Inspector and said, "How about lunch some day soon?"

"Sounds good to me! I'll need to celebrate after cracking this case. I'll call you." Adams left smiling.

* * *

While Inspector Adams was working on his theory and waiting for an answer from Myron Cooke, Mary continued her mission on getting her body back to normal.

Between her occasional trips back to the office where she spent an hour or two each day and the equipment room at the YWCA, Mary's week went by fast. But Helen Randall, the brooch and Inspector Adams roamed through her thoughts regularly. She decided to call Michael Bromley.

"Michael, this is Mary Bryant." It was high time for her to drop the Clark. She didn't need a reminder of Peter Clark or his family any longer. Two days before she had driven the Dodge Dart over to the Rockford Court House to make all the necessary changes.

"Yes, Mary. How are you doing?" said Michael.

"I'm much better and improving each day, thank you. I have some information about the Clark family I'd like to share with you. Can we set up an appointment?"

Michael asked Mary to meet him at his

office the following morning at nine o'clock. She presented Michael with the same facts that she shared with Reed and Grace previously. She emphasized the fact that Karen could be involved because of her anger when Peter gave the brooch to her. Karen made several comments to her on why the brooch should have been kept in the family. Mary brought to light that even though Helen desired the brooch, she may not be involved in the burglary.

Michael listened attentively. Then asked, "How about Frank Knight, Mary, do you think he's involved?"

Mary thought a moment before answering. "He could be for the simple reason we think he's the only one who knew the code numbers. He had to have shared it with the burglar, unless his secretary knew the code to the safe, and she passed it on."

Michael stored Mary's comment in the back of his mind. After she left, he called Frank Knight. His secretary answered saying he was out of the office today and would be back tomorrow.

* * *

While Mary drove home, she thought about Reed. He had been extremely busy lately catching up on breaking news that streamed into the headlines about a fire that damaged a home on the east side of Rockford. Two children were left alone while parents drank at the corner bar. A boy eight-years-old and a girl five were found in their beds dead from smoke inhalation. Investigations were ongoing and the newspapers were filled with reports.

Although they talked by phone several times during the week, It had been a while since Mary saw him. As she pulled the car into the garage, she decided to invite him over for a special evening. She had some making up to do after her cranky behavior while she was recuperating from surgery. She assured Grace she was well enough to handle a dinner in the kitchen, so all preparations were made by her, except the dessert. She turned that over to her mother, who was excellent at preparing some of Reed's favorites. When Grace finished the dessert, she called her friend who had invited her to stay the night.

Knowing Reed loved a good steak, Mary decided that's exactly what she would serve along with twice baked potatoes, steamed asparagus, salad and hot rolls; another of his favorites. She kept a catalog of gourmet wines for years on her magazine rack. After carefully scanning the list of fine wines, she selected a bottle of Ravenswood red Zinfandel. She stopped at a liquor store on her way home from the park and chilled it immediately.

Nineteen

*M*ary called Reed and invited him to dinner. He arrived around 7:30, with a bouquet of red roses. To his surprise, she answered the door; usually Grace did. Her black spaghetti strap dress clung in all the right places, and he never knew a foot could be so beautiful in a black thin strapped sandal. Mary's hair, now shoulder length, was crimson with light sparkles floating through it, highlighting her dramatic blue eyes that always mesmerized Reed. He stood speechless and just stared.

Mary accepted the roses and closed the door softly behind him. She kissed him tenderly on the lips. He wanted more, but she took his hand and led him into the kitchen. While she placed the roses in a vase of water, Reed opened the bottle of wine. Thinking how perfectly adorable he was, she retrieved two goblets from the freezer and Reed poured the wine. In this time, nothing was said between them, only their eyes told a story. He knew something was up since Grace was nowhere to be found, and he never asked. After a few sips of wine apiece, Mary led Reed to the bedroom. Her bedroom, generally bright and cheery, was now subdued and romantic with lighted candles and closed drapes. Reed slipped the spaghetti straps down off her shoulders slowly, kissed her neck, nose and lips gently with all his heart, knowing for the first time in his life, he had found his true love.

Passion increased between them leaving nothing to chance or another time. She found the emotional balance needed in his arms and he knew he would love her forever.

After dinner, Reed and Mary donned heavy coats and went out to sit around the willow tree. Mary had grabbed the blanket hanging over a chair she and Grace always had handy on a winter night, and Reed carried their goblets and the bottle of wine. Together, they cuddled on the chase lounge and talked about many incidents in their past life. Mary gave him more detail on her marriage to Peter and Reed wondered out loud why he even thought a relationship with Cheryl would work. They drank more wine and talked for hours avoiding other matters and topics, only using the time for each other. Once more, they returned to Mary's bedroom where Reed's heart overflowed with love when he asked, "Mary will you marry me?"

When she answered "yes," she felt his

body tremble.

* * *

Inspector Adams was convinced that Helen Randall did not arrange the burglary, but not convinced that Frank Knight didn't have anything to do with it. As he pondered this assumption, the phone rang. It was Myron Cooke.

"Inspector, you are a very lucky man to get a report on your button so quickly. Three days is unbelievable around here. But it seems the Lab Department liked black satin also."

"Well, I appreciate the special attention," answered Adams with a smile in his voice. "What have you got for me?"

"We assume the thumb print belongs to a young woman, but that's about all we can determine. Because the button is so small, only the tip of a thumb print is obvious. The lab feels it is more likely a glove button than a blouse because it is so tiny. It must have been torn off after catching on to something. If you had the article the button was torn from, that would be a different story. We could determine if the broken threads match each other, which would allow us to give you better evidence. Sorry we can't tell you more now. Robert, my assistant, is coming over to Police Headquarters with some samples. Should I send the button with him?"

"I would appreciate that, Myron. I'll be here for another hour or so. Thanks for the tip on the matching threads."

"Will do, Inspector, and good luck on your investigation,"

"Thanks for your help, Myron."

Robert arrived within a half hour after Adams talked to Myron Cooke. The Inspector checked his watch and saw that it was five o'clock. He put the manila envelope in his coat pocket and placed a call to Helen Randall.

"Mrs. Randall, this is Inspector Adams. Could I drop by? I have a piece of evidence I would like to show you."

"Yes, Inspector, that would be fine if it doesn't take too long. We have a dinner engagement this evening."

Twenty minutes later, Inspector Adams pulled in behind a black Malibu in Helen Randall's driveway. He gave some serious thought to the Malibu, remembering what Tom Conklin said about the other car in the parking lot of Frank Knight's office building, but avoided jumping to conclusions. Adams walked up the path to the front door and rang the bell.

Rose answered. "Come in please."

She led the Inspector to the back study where Helen was in conversation with a guest.

He could hear her say, "We will probably have about 150 people."

As Inspector Adams entered the room, Helen lifted her head and said, "Come in, Inspector. I'll be with you in a minute." Helen's guest turned around to see who came in.

"Karen, this is Inspector Adams with the Police Department. He's investigating the burglary at Frank Knight's office. Inspector, this is my daughter, Karen. We are planning a party. Now, what is it you wanted to show me?"

Adams eyes focused on the pretty woman, who resembled her mother, with brown hair and green eyes, dressed smartly in a black silk suit with a yellow blouse. She nodded as they were introduced, but said nothing.

As Karen lifted a pair of black gloves from her purse she said, "I have to be going now, Mother. We can talk about this again tomorrow."

Helen watched as Karen started to apply a glove to one hand. In a concerned voice she said, "Karen, you have a button missing from your glove."

"Oh dear, now where did that go."

Inspector Adams' eyes flew quickly to the other glove in her hand and he saw that the button matched the one in his pocket.

Removing the manila envelope from his pocket, he shook the button into the palm of his hand. "Is this what you're looking for?"

Karen withdrew inwardly. The terrified look on her face told all.

Inspector Adams took her by the arm, "We have some questions to ask you, Madam." He escorted her out the front door listening to her objections. Helen Randall stood wide-eyed and stunned, trying desperately to absorb what had just happened.

Adams called Police Chief Dan Berry on his car phone. "We'll be there shortly. She's handcuffed and has been read her rights. Can you stick around to help me question her?"

* * *

Karen entered the police department protesting.

"Mrs. Mosley, *please* be seated," said Chief Berry pointing to the chair next to his desk "and be quiet."

Karen continued her outcry. "I want my lawyer and I want to call my husband. There are a lot of similar buttons out there, and you can't prove that one button came from my glove. Why, my daughter has a button just like that on a black blouse she owns," said Karen sarcastically.

"Should we consider your daughter to be

the guilty person, Mrs. Mosley?" asked Chief Berry.

Both the Inspector and the Chief were stunned that she'd involve her daughter.

Karen stared in silence.

Adams wanted to get to the truth, but yet he wanted to calm her. There was a chance she might be innocent. From her appearance, no one would ever suspect her of any criminal behavior, but he knew how much the brooch meant to the women in the family. Somehow this burglary was concocted between two people who thought they could get away with it. He felt sure Karen was one of the two, but it may be harder to catch the other thief.

Karen was allowed to call her lawyer, but she called her mother instead. Helen Randall called Clifford Lakes, *her* lawyer. Clifford, about thirty-two, five feet ten inches tall, admired and even thought of as handsome with black hair, blue eyes and sharp ties, took the case on exactly what Karen had said. "There are a lot of similar buttons out there. You can't prove it came from my glove. Another thing, I picked these up on a store table that contained several gloves of the same design. Someone else could have lost the button."

Chief Berry asked Karen to show the matching glove. Both gloves were laid on the chief's desk. No two ways about it, the buttons matched. Chief Berry looked up and stared at Inspector Adams. Adams knew he had his thief. He had her glove and the button. He checked his watch. Six o'clock, time for dinner. He would call Myron Cooke in the morning.

Karen shouted out again. "Listen, I've been in Wisconsin for two weeks visiting friends and relatives. I wore the gloves often because of the cold weather. I must have lost the button there. I've never been in Frank Knight's office. And furthermore, I don't even know where his safe is let alone how to open it. You have the wrong person. I'm not saying another word until you talk to my lawyer."

Helen Randall paid the $10,000 bail. Karen was released and told to appear in court in one month.

Twenty

"*K*aren, are you telling me the truth?" asked Clifford Lakes as they sat in Helen's luxurious living room.

"Of course, I'm telling ·you the truth," said Karen boldly. "I'm a victim more than a criminal. I don't even know Frank Knight and yet, I'm being accused of assisting him in a burglary. Is there something wrong here?"

Clifford was convinced. This lady is innocent. His next step was to call Frank Knight.

Frank answered the phone on the third ring.

"I'm Clifford Lakes, Karen Clark Mosley's lawyer, Mr. Knight. This morning's Register Star newspaper carried an article on her arrest for the burglary that took place in your office. I would like to talk to you before the police arrive. They may be knocking at your door any time now. I assume you saw your name mentioned as an accomplice." Clifford said tapping his desk with a pencil.

"I don't know what you're talking about. Do you really think I would have someone rob my own safe," answered Frank.

"Maybe not, Mr. Knight, but I would like to ask you some questions. Could I come by this afternoon around two?"

Frank agreed and the call ended.

At the same time, Karen sat at her dressing table sipping a glass of red wine. Mitch Mosley, Karen's husband called earlier to say his boss was having an evening cocktail party. "Get ready. We'll leave around six thirty," he said.

She had pulled her black hair off her forehead with a head band and began to apply makeup. She stopped to stare into the mirror, worry lines were showing. Should she tell Mitch the whole story? The theft was not going according to plan and, somehow, she might be the fall guy in this whole setup. What to do? Frank Knight would lie. He's been a lying lawyer for years and would get away with it again. Peter should have never given that brooch to Mary. Mother could have treasured it for a while, but I'm sure she would have willed it to me. She knew how much it meant to me. Mary didn't deserve it.

She broke Peter's heart when she divorced him. I will have to convince that annoying Inspector, Mother's lawyer, and the judge that a button is not enough evidence to convict me.

Twenty-one

*T*he first thing Adams did after leaving the police station was call Myron Cooke. "Myron, this is Adams. I'd like to bring the glove over to you that had the missing button. Would you be there in about fifteen minutes?"

"Yes, Inspector, I plan on being here for about another hour. Come on over."

Myron eyed both the button threads and the threads from the glove on the slab. He removed his glasses, looked up at Adams and said, "I think you have your thief. But, to confirm, I'll have the lab people check it out in the morning. Is that soon enough?"

Adams had been looking over Myron's shoulder. He walked around the counter, placed his elbows on the edge, smiled and said, "That will be just fine."

Having finished his business, the instructor hurried back to his office. The phone was ringing when he opened his door. He lifted the receiver. "Adams here!"

"Inspector Adams, this is Tom Conklin. I'm sorry I didn't call you sooner, but I just found the license number of that black

Malibu you needed. Would you believe I found it mixed in with a client's file? I pulled the file this morning and. . . .

"Yes, yes, Mr. Conklin, just give me the number."

"Oh yes, of course, it's KM4219 and it had a road runner in the corner."

"Mr. Adams, are you there?"

The line was dead.

Inspector Adams' blood was sizzling. His case was almost solved. All he needed was a call from Myron or the lab confirming that the threads on the glove and button matched. He remembered that exact license plate number when he saw Karen Mosley's car in Helen Randall's driveway just days ago.

His wish was granted when Myron called his office the following morning. "Perfect match," was all he said.

"Thanks Myron. I'll call you for lunch. Treats on me."

* * *

Adams used another approach on Frank Knight. Instead of calling, he arrived at his office soon after Knight's phone conversation with Karen's lawyer. His secretary buzzed him and Frank, caught off guard, consented to see him.

Frank stood up, shook hands and said, "Inspector."

"Appreciate your seeing me, Mr. Knight. You've been cited as an accomplice to this burglary and before the police get here to take you to headquarters, I wanted to present you with some facts that have come to light."

"Like what?" asked Frank. "I'll tell you the same thing I told Karen's lawyer, *the great Clifford Lakes.* I had nothing to do with this crime. Do you think I'd have my own safe robbed?

Inspector Adams took his time answering Frank. "The way I see it, Karen Mosley was going to pay you a pretty penny to help her get the brooch. The idea that you two came up with was that the robber and brooch would disappear and, with time, the whole thing would be forgotten, and you two would go your merry way. But, you see, Mr. Knight, there was one thing I didn't tell you. Tom Conklin is an excellent lawyer and he never looks at suspicious cars without writing down the license plate numbers. It has been confirmed that Karen Mosley owns a black Malibu and since the rear of her car was facing Tom's window while you were chatting with her in the parking lot on the night of the robbery, he jotted down the license plate number. We now have a perfect match, Karen's car to Tom's license plate number. Quite a coincidence, don't you think?"

Adams followed up with, "Sit tight Mr. Knight. Don't move because there are two police cars pulling into the parking lot of your building right this very minute."

Within minutes two burly police officers entered the office. As they handcuffed Frank, his secretary sat stunned at her desk. Frank turned to her and said, "Cancel all my appointments for this afternoon."

Police Chief Dan Berry laughed and said, "You better cancel tomorrow's appointments, too." Two other cops accompanying the police chief laughed as well.

Clifford Lakes arrived at two o'clock and after Frank's secretary relayed what had happened earlier, he left frantic. He slipped into his Cadillac and called Karen on his car phone. The Nanny answered and said she was not available. He soon found out that Karen had been brought in again for questioning.

After Inspector Adams ran through his diatribe to Karen on her license plate matching the number Tom Conklin jotted down, and the fact that her glove and button threads matched, she confessed. She expressed anger in not having the brooch willed to her in the first place instead of Peter, and explained that she needed Frank Knight to help gain possession of the brooch. She told Police Chief Berry that she was willing to pay him well for his help in obtaining the brooch. Frank Knight and Karen Mosley are sitting in jail waiting on a trial date and the judge's decision.

Not only did The Lowell Report newspaper carry the story on the front page, but the Register Star and The Journal Standard as well. Rockford's residents buzzed with gossip as they grocery shopped, put gas in their cars and attended theaters. Frank Knight always worried them since his track record wasn't the greatest, but to have Helen Randall's daughter actually involved in a crime was truly juicy news.

Mitch Mosley, Karen's husband, was shocked when he learned that the judge gave Karen a year in jail and one year of community service. All this scheming and stealing had gone on without his knowledge. He was amazed.

* * *

When Grace and Mary heard the whole story from Inspector Adams, both agreed neither of them wanted anything that belonged to the Randall family. Mary gave both items back to Helen Randall with the condition they never bother her again. She immediately threw herself into planning her own wedding, instead of writing about someone else's.

"Reed, I'm so glad this mess is all over," she said in a phone conversation with him. Why don't you come over after work for a good dinner? I'd like to talk about our wedding plans. Is that okay with you?"

"That's is fine with me, Mary, but how about keeping it simple?"

"I'm glad to hear you say that. It's exactly what I have in mind."

Carol Langley, the current society writer for The Lowell Report, not only interviewed Mary for details on her wedding, but was assigned Cheryl Cunningham's wedding. Cheryl had met Michael Bromley through Helen Randall's lawyer, Clifford Lakes, at a social event held regularly in Rockford. Love bloomed after they dated six months. They were married November 21st, a few days before Thanksgiving, and all of Cheryl's dreams for a huge, affluent wedding were realized.

Since it was a second marriage for Mary, she felt completely content with a private home reception and a simple, ceremony in the quaint, but beautiful, Allen Chapel on Winnebago Avenue three days before Christmas. Reed's mother, Phoebe and Grace served as attendants and few close *Lowell Report* employees were invited to a reception at Grace's home.

"Mother, are you sure the wedding plans will not be too exhausting for you if we have the reception at home?" Mary asked her mother early one morning.

"No, not at all," said Grace. I intend to call the cleaning service I had last year when my charity club had their fund raiser here at our house. I hope to get Jeannie and Michelle again. They were wonderful and, they not only clean, but offer information on many catering shops in Rockford that prepare wedding cakes and appetizers. You and Reed can take care of the alcoholic drinks"

One week before the wedding, Grace presented Reed and Mary with the deed to her house as a gift to be effective when they returned from a honeymoon in the Bahamas.

"It's senseless for you to look for an apartment or another house when this is available, if you want it." Grace said.

Mary turned to Reed, smiled, shrugged her shoulders and said, "Reed?"

"Only on one condition," said Reed mischievously "if Grace does the cooking."

Mary poked him in the ribs.